KNUTE, AND KNUTE AGAIN

KNUTE, AND KNUTE AGAIN

A NOVEL BY WILLIAM WARNER

ALGONQUIN BOOKS OF CHAPEL HILL 1987

Published by
Algonquin Books of Chapel Hill
Post Office Box 2225
Chapel Hill, North Carolina 27515-2225

in association with
Taylor Publishing Company
1550 West Mockingbird Lane
Dallas, Texas 75235

LIBRARY OF CONGRESS CATALOGING-IN-PUBLICATION DATA
Warner, William, 1954–
Knute, and Knute again.

I. Title.
PS3573.A768K55   1987   813'.54   86-26481
ISBN 0-912697-53-9

This book is dedicated to three very important people:
Sam Warner, my father; Lyle Warner, my mother;
and Molly Renda-Warner, my wife.

KNUTE, AND KNUTE AGAIN

Chapter 1

When Knute, whose name I pronounce "newt" with a silent *K*—when he was in the fourth grade he broke a girl's arm. On purpose?

Not really, not exactly, I'll say. Of course you will do your own judging after you've heard the whole story. The school nurse listed the event behind the divider in her notebook with the tab *Accidents, Playground*.

The girl, whose name was Toni, had her arm set in a cast; four weeks later it functioned as before. She was in pain until the cast was put on and she was given some aspirin. After a few weeks she had no memory of this pain. While she was partially incapacitated her friends at school and her mother at home were constantly offering to do things for her—carry her books, do her homework, brush her long hair, draw on her cast, sit with her during lunch. Her older brother was assigned double duty on the dishes. At first she enjoyed her special status, all the other kids greeting her, seeming so concerned about her. After a few days this seemed tiresome, she missed her usual, less prominent position.

Knute wished that, after special events like this, you could go talk to someone, appeal to them. See if they couldn't just change the result a little. It had only been a matter of inches, he believed. An inch more left or right, or maybe his shoulder not hitting her square in the middle of her back, and she would have been OK. Maybe she would have just had some scrapes on her knees and elbows, or something. And then he wouldn't have had to feel so guilty, have the assistant principal on his case.

His mother suggested he give Toni a present, and so he went with his mother to the department store at the local shopping center and watched her pick out a silvery bracelet with brown stones for Toni to wear after the cast came off. In class sometimes he would look over at Toni where she sat at her desk one row back and two across to his right. Going out to recess or lunch, or out on the playground, he often stayed near her. A few yards off, not quite in her group. Glancing at her suspiciously, the way some children will look suspiciously at new students, or students of different races or cultures. Where had she come from? he wondered. Why did she always come to school with her right arm covered in white plaster? Why couldn't she see that the other students in his class didn't dress that way? Perhaps if she would ask him to join her group, or have lunch or walk home from school with her—he'd tell her. What? Maybe they could just walk together, talk about Miss Osterhaut, their teacher.

Toni's friends would drive him off. Step between him and

her. Cross their arms in front of their chests. Shout: "Bully!" "You stay away from Toni!" "She doesn't want you looking at her!"

But Toni would smile and make little waving motions that she had been taught were cute, endearing. If her friends had left her momentarily unguarded, she'd step over and talk with Knute. She said to him many times that, in her opinion, he hadn't been at fault, she didn't blame him or hate him. One time she apologized for her friends, explaining that—since they'd been on the other side of the fence—they had misunderstood how it had happened.

"They don't understand it was an accident," Knute said. Toni agreed completely.

Knute and Toni both came to enjoy the sense that they alone and apart from the rest of their friends and classmates had been the participants in a significant event, and to like the roles their memories of this event offered them. Knute felt powerful, and unduly put upon by bad luck. Toni was wounded but not angry. She comforted Knute and felt sorry because she, by breaking her arm, had caused him to feel sorry. Together they cursed their luck and laughed. Toni proposed and Knute, suppressing his doubts, said he agreed: Their accident hadn't been caused by either of them. It was the combination. Of her dumbness and his being smart. Her putting out her arm to stop herself from falling—which their gym teacher must have told them a thousand million times not to do. And then just Knute's not putting out his arm, so he ended up falling on top of her.

In the late spring, a few months after the event, Toni proposed and Knute agreed that they were boyfriend and girl-friend. One morning they took a bus to the shopping center and bought each other rings. She went to all his Little League games and twice, on his mother's invitation, came swimming over at the pool in his backyard. Mrs. Pescadoor made them lunch and the three of them ate together, sitting on the terrace in the black metal chairs there; Mrs. Pescadoor at the table, Knute agreeing with Toni both times that they preferred to eat with their plates on their laps.

His mother did most of the talking. He kept glancing over at Toni, trying to catch her off guard, to find out what she was really thinking, to see that in fact she despised him. But every time she would sense his glance and turn her head and smile, with apparent warmth and pleasure. She giggled and then he giggled, and then they both giggled, hearing the sounds of one another eating potato chips. She noticed that he had noticed her feet swinging under her chair, and then smiled. In the car going home she held his hand.

The romance didn't last. That August, as every August when he was growing up, Knute and his mother went to his grandparents' cabin, two states away. It didn't occur to either him or Toni to write letters while he was gone, and in the fall, basically they'd forgotten about one another. They were just classmates, a boy and a girl at an age when the two sexes tended to keep a certain distance. The next year she and her family moved out West.

Which is not to say Toni has disappeared completely from

Knute's life. He retained memories of her fourth-grade self, their fourth-grade intimacy. And many years later, nights lying in bed in his college dorm room in the East, hundreds of miles from home, finding a use for such memories . . . Quite a few nights Knute fell asleep with Toni.

He has come, as an adult, to appoint Toni the first girl in his life. That is (to attempt a definition): The girl from when he was youngest to whom he remembers being attracted and for whom he can remember a name, plus some images or physical details, though not necessarily accurate ones. Small, he is pretty sure she was small for her age, with thin, very thin wrists. He can see her long, light brown hair, her friends brushing it, putting it into a ponytail. Small features—small ears, small nose. He has more the idea that she was small, even for her age, than he has a picture of what she looked like.

During his short baseball career he was a third baseman. And he remembers how at his games she used to sit on the top bench of the stands and at the far end, all the way up the third base line, so she'd be close to him when he was in the field and far away when he was at the plate. She said, more than once, and he still doesn't question it: She was afraid of him being hit by a ball and killed when he was up at bat.

Lying in bed at college, he began to see her as he had not been able to when he had been busy with his games (somewhat concerned himself about being hit by a pitch or, equally annoying, dropping a high pop-up). She wears white shorts—gym shorts essentially, cotton with an elastic waistband. She is up on her perch at the top and far end of the bench, her very thin, very bare, very light brown legs pressed together at the knees. Her little, very thin-boned jaw clenched. Those little, tiny hands he has held, stuck way up into the crotch of those shorts.

Which is not to say he has forgotten he broke her arm. Some nights when Knute was at college he would find himself up late talking with a female classmate. The past was a popular subject. Where did you go to high school? In the Midwest? What is it really like out there? And then, perhaps: What were you like as a kid? What did you used to like to do? What were your favorite TV shows? What is *the first thing* you can remember? (We're getting more intimate now.) What was your first girlfriend like? What was the *worst* thing you can ever remember doing?

Sometimes Knute would talk about this incident. When he was in the fourth grade he had broken a girl's arm. (The joke is that there he was, alone with a girl to whom he was attracted and who was attracted to him. It was late at night; they were talking intimately about their pasts, getting to know one another; trying to decide how intimate they wanted to or were willing to be; whether, when or how often they were going to have sexual intercourse—Knute comes right out with the most violent thing he'd ever done to a female. But, of course, neither he nor the young women with whom he talked ever got the joke.)

*

So how did he break this poor girl's arm?

Knute likes to use his matter-of-fact, disinterested tone

when telling the story. "I broke the girl's arm chasing her, trying to catch her. There was a race—we were racing. A group of girls had been taunting me during recess, and finally I just started running after them. When I caught up to Toni I broke her arm. Not intentionally—I fell on her—and she stuck out her arm. An error in judgment."

Why were the girls taunting you though?

"Oh, just because I had had to go to the assistant principal's office that morning. That gave them their opening, something they could tease me about. About how I'd gotten caught, or punished."

Why did you have to go to the assistant principal's though? What did you do that you had to be punished for?

(Thanks to this story and the way he tells it, one female has gone to bed with him. This girl—a Susan—stands as the first girl in his life in another sense: She was the first girl at his college with whom he had sex. Many of the other girls and women he has told the story to . . . Well, in many cases, owing to such things as marriage and timidity, sex has not even been a possibility. But many females, much as the ten-year-old Toni, have smiled a lot. They have used phrases like "What a sad story!" And, "Oh, I can't believe what you had to go through!" Some of them have enjoyed the idea of Knute as a child violating rules, being punished. When *they* have been lying in bed, going through *their* mental souvenirs, they have found uses for images of Knute in the fourth grade, sitting in an assistant principal's office . . .)

"I had to go to the assistant principal's office because I was late to school. It was a test. I'd been coming late with some

7

regularity, so the assistant principal set up this test. If I came late again I had to go to his office for the first period. Failing the test, I had to go to his office."

And were you often late to school as a kid?

"Me, personally? That one year I suppose you'd have to say I arrived late fairly often. But, of course, it was complicated."

*

Two notes. First, Knute was never a particularly punctual student. Even as an adult—working in a library, then driving limousines, then opening first a sporting goods store, then one kind of restaurant popular among a certain West Coast crowd, and now another kind of restaurant popular among a higher-income West Coast crowd—he can be counted on to drive up late, glance quickly right at the eyes of those who have been waiting for him, silently raising and setting aside two questions: They didn't really expect him to be on time, did they? They weren't really going to waste everybody's time being angry at him for being a few minutes late?

Second, it *is* complicated. I am the writer and this is fiction, so (it should be simple) if things get too complicated I should be able to simplify them. But, in part through working on this novel, I have been taught that simplification doesn't interest me as much as complexity.

*

Just a few blocks from the house in which Knute's mother grew up there was a small pond where as a child winter afternoons and weekends she often went skating. "Every day after school," it is in her memory. And as an adult she recalls fondly a certain variation on hockey that her brothers and their friends played, using a special kind of smooth, flat rock. To her sons, daughter, husband, adult friends she has made it known that some of the happiest days of her life were spent playing this game with her brothers. A part of her knows though that usually it was just for a few minutes, or at best for a half-hour, until another male showed up and they could have even teams without her.

When Knute was a child, during the winter when the municipal rink in his suburb was open, many afternoons when he came out of his school building his mother would be waiting for him. The station wagon idling in the circular drive. As an adult *he* recalls his mother standing in the middle of that drive so that mothers who already had their children in their cars couldn't drive away. A lot of honking.

When he got in the car, often his skates were on the front seat next to his mother's. She wanted to know how he felt about going skating. Knute had not gotten the idea that it was important for him to determine or imagine an answer to that question. Often he said nothing, and his mother would continue, "I'm dying to go skating and get outdoors. Do you realize, until just now, getting in the car to come get you—I haven't been outside all day. I've hardly been out of the kitchen. I . . ." By the time she'd finished her description of her day's activities, sitting at her table in the kitchen, trying to write a letter to one of her sisters or whatever—they'd be looking for a parking space on one of the streets near the rink.

They'd skate for a few hours, racing one another, playing tag or trying to get the rink supervisor to *worry* that perhaps they were racing or playing tag and, therefore, violating the posted rules, interfering with the other skaters' enjoyment of the facilities, frightening and endangering little children. . . . But not being so obvious that this supervisor felt he had the right to kick them off the ice for the day.

Did Knute enjoy these afternoons—or the weekend outings when his mother would take him to the local college rink or, if it had been cold enough, to a local pond? He didn't *not* enjoy them, and you could say he hadn't yet had enough free time to grasp that his mother's tastes and schedule weren't necessarily his. In the winter after school and on weekends he often went skating with his mother. Then often, afternoons, they'd go to the supermarket, come home and cook themselves dinner, wash up; and then they'd sit at the dining table working together on his homework. This was Knute's winter life, and he was too young to make such a definition. He was just living the life.

Since before Knute's family moved to the town, there had been the two rinks: the relatively small, outdoor, municipal rink, and, at the local state college field house, a larger, indoor rink which on the weekends was open to community residents. And then the college expanded and the field house got to be fifteen, twenty years old, and, when Knute was in the first grade, work was begun on an arena that was to be equipped with a still larger indoor rink.

Occasionally during the few years it was under construction,

Knute's mother had driven him over to the site. She had taken him up the slope to the entrance into the work area to watch the men and machines in the pit below; the concrete slowly building up on the sides, forming the stands; caves for locker rooms, hallways; scaffolding rising up from the center as work began on the roof. When the arena was almost done, one afternoon they watched the crew of painters bent over and working steadily around, painting the benches yellow. "Sometimes I just think I'm blessed!" Knute's mother said.

Knute looked up at her as if not comprehending.

"We move here—we could have moved to so many different suburbs—but we came here. And now they're building this rink. Did I tell you I read in the paper that some of the equipment they've got is the most modern in the world?"

"You know it's not just a rink?" Knute asked, concerned his mother wasn't aware of this fact.

"Oh yeah, I know," she said. "That's part of the modern equipment they're going to have. In just one hour they're going to be able to change the surface from ice to a basketball court, or back the other way."

"The ice is always there," Knute said.

"Oh yeah, I know. That's how they make it work. The floor is going to be like a jigsaw puzzle that they just lay on top, with some padding so the players' feet don't get too cold."

Mrs. Pescadoor, Knute's mother, wanted to skate at the new rink. But it was not open to the public. But there was a boy, Doug Levitt, Knute's age, with whom the Pescadoors had become friends. He was often at the municipal rink afternoons, and Mrs. Pescadoor had invited him to join in their games, to come skating with them on weekends, to come over for dinner. A few times Doug's father and the three of them had gone into the city to see the National Hockey League team play.

Mr. Levitt was in charge of public relations for the college, and Mrs. Pescadoor asked him a number of times if he could get her, Doug and Knute a special pass to use the rink. For over a year Mr. Levitt said no, it just wasn't something he could do. Then at a cocktail party he found himself talking with the wife of the president of the college. Mr. Levitt reported how anxious his son and two of his son's friends were to get a chance to skate at the new rink. Two afternoons later Doug brought to the municipal rink a letter from the president giving Doug Levitt, Knute Pescadoor and Virginia Pescadoor permission to use the rink weekday mornings before the college hockey team's practices.

Mrs. Pescadoor outlined the plan for the initial sortie. When they got home that afternoon, the two Pescadoors would call Doug and they'd "synchronize their watches" (their alarm clocks). Each of them would set their alarms for 5:30. Whoever of the three got up first would either look in on or call the others, to make sure they were up. By 6:00 Knute and his mother would be in front of Doug's house ready to take him to the rink. By 6:15 they'd be on the ice. By 7:00 off, and Mrs. Pescadoor would take them all to a nearby restaurant for breakfast and then to school.

The next morning they did this, or at least the beginning of it. And it did have the aura of a secret mission. Getting up before dawn; no one else out except one dog, one police car and one paperboy. The streetlights still on, the traffic lights off.

They were the first skaters to arrive at the arena. The way it was built—sunk in the ground—visitors walked up a slight rise from the parking area and then entered at the top of the stands. So, when Knute, Doug and Mrs. Pescadoor entered they saw all the curving, glossy yellow benches of the stands empty beneath them. Not one person on one bench. Far below the two maintenance men just finishing cleaning the ice. A thin layer of water gleaming on the surface.

"Whaa-hoo! Whaa-hoo!" Doug shouted. New ice and nobody on it and a whole arena all to themselves. He went running down to the rink.

"Whaa-hoo! Whaa-hoo!" Knute's mother shouted and ran after him. "This is going to be great! Isn't this perfect! I told you it was going to be perfect. Now aren't you glad you got up so early?" She turned back to look up at Knute, hopping down the steps after the two of them. His head down, counting how many hops it was taking him to get all the way to the bottom. "Now aren't you glad you got up so early!" she repeated.

He nodded without looking up, trying not to lose count.

They skated and skated, all up and down and around the ice. They made patterns with their skates on the new ice and played tag. Mrs. Pescadoor struck up a conversation with one of the maintenance men which led to him bringing them out three hockey sticks and a puck. She tried to get him to put in one of the goals as well, but he said he wasn't allowed to do that.

According to the rules they weren't even allowed to have sticks and a puck on the ice during "open skating." But since only a few other skaters had come, as long as they stayed out of the other people's way he said he thought it would be OK. Doug got his sneakers and they used those to make a goal. The three of them rotated—one played goalie, the other two were a team, trying to get the puck past the goalie. When they succeeded, another person became the goalie.

The plan had them off the ice at 7:00, on to breakfast and school. But neither Knute nor his mother ever paid much attention to time, and Doug was so excited he lost track. When the maintenance men came over and said they had to get off so he could clean the ice again for the hockey team practice, Doug said, "What time is it!" When the man said 8:10, Doug and Mrs. Pescadoor said almost in unison, "You've gotta be kidding!"

Doug became quite worried. He was already late to school! He just couldn't be late to school because his teacher was very strict. In his class, he said, if you were late and you didn't have a note from your parents or a doctor, you had to follow the teacher out to recess and stay sitting next to her. If you tried to get up at all, say just to get a ball for somebody if it went over near you—if you just stood up—she'd reach up her hand, grab your sleeve, and yank you back down next to her. One time she had even torn a friend of his' baseball jacket. A jacket the kid's father had just gotten for him. With the name of the city's baseball team on the front. His friend had just stood up for ten seconds to go get a ball and the teacher had yanked him back down so hard it had made a rip in his jacket. And she didn't even apologize.

"That's terrible," Knute's mother said flatly, her thoughts elsewhere.

"And I'm already late," Doug said.

"And we haven't had our breakfast yet," Mrs. Pescadoor said. "I promised you kids I was going to take you out to eat."

We don't have time for that now, Knute and Doug both said. But Mrs. Pescadoor said she had thought of a solution to all their problems. They'd go to the restaurant, each have a big plate of pancakes with bacon and orange juice—or have eggs if any of them preferred. They'd take their time. And when they were ready to go to school she'd write each of the boys a note saying they had a doctor's appointment.

Doug looked at Knute to get his opinion. Knute shrugged, Why not? "OK, fine," Doug said.

The three of them changed out of their skates and went to the restaurant, ordered their big breakfasts. They got the morning paper. Mrs. Pescadoor read them their horoscopes and worked on the crossword puzzle and the acrostic. Doug took the sports page, spread it out on the table and bent down close to it like a textile buyer examining a fabric for inconsistencies. Periodically he'd look over at Knute and pass along some data—one star hockey player had gotten a "hat trick" the previous night; one National Hockey League team had fallen way behind in the standings. The news excited Doug. "Can you believe that! That's his third hat trick already this season!" he said. And, "Can you believe they're already thirty-seven points behind? Incredible!"

Knute nodded agreeably. His mother took him to hockey games, and to baseball and football games; she often wanted him to watch sports on television with her Saturday afternoons. She, Doug and the kids at school often talked about sports. As, at least in theory, elevator passengers find muzak, so Knute found the games and conversation a pleasant enough, calming diversion, though he never had any need to pin down such things as who this star player was or what thirty-seven points represented. That morning in the restaurant he over-dosed his pancakes with syrup and spent a good twenty minutes carving off segments of the stacks and sloshing those segments around in the lake of syrup. He hardly ate any of the food; he watched the cars going by on the road, a car salesman on the lot next door, in a light blue suit, with tight blond curls, going from car to car on the lot, opening and closing doors, making sure the interiors were clean.

"Blank to the wise," his mother said loudly at one point, ending Knute's surveillance of the car salesman. "Blank to the wise. That's the clue, now one of you two has to guess what the blank is. What word is it *really*? I've already figured it out, but I'm giving you this as a test. It's a test of how *smart* you are."

Blank to the wise? Doug looked at Knute who shrugged and said, "Wise guys to the wise?"

"How about 'wizards to the wise'?" Doug asked. "War to the wise!"

Mrs. Pescadoor kept shaking her head. "Not even close. You're not even close."

Dauntless, Doug kept making new proposals. "Diamonds to the wise? Gold to the wise?"

16

Knute had played this game with his mother many times without noticeable success, and he had lost the little interest he had had in coming up with the right answer. He said nothing for a long time, and then, as if after much calculation, he said, "I think I've got it."

"What!" Doug asked.

"I'm sure he doesn't have it, Doug," Mrs. Pescadoor said, as familiar with her son's games as he was with hers.

Knute gave his very soggy pancakes a definitive jab with his fork, then looked up and said, "Never whisper to the wise."

"Oh, that's not it! That can't be it," Doug said. "Is that it?"

Mrs. Pescadoor shook her head. "I told you he didn't have it, Doug." She smiled affectionately at her son who had his head bent sheepishly. "He's like his father. He just tries to pull your leg. He never even bothers to try and guess."

By 9:30 Mrs. Pescadoor had finished her third cup of coffee and her fourth cigarette. Doug had long since finished with the sports section. Mrs. Pescadoor had proposed a few more crossword puzzle clues to which Doug had made his many excited and hopeful guesses, Knute his one or two quiet and silly suggestions. Mrs. Pescadoor borrowed the waitress's pen and wrote out two almost identical notes: My son, Knute or Doug, had to go to a doctor's appointment this morning. Please excuse the delay this has caused in getting him to your class. Thank you very much. Sincerely yours, [respectively] Mrs. Nicholas Pescadoor and Mrs. Frank Levitt.

A few days later the threesome went to the rink again before school, although this time Doug kept his eye on the clock and suggested they not take so long at breakfast. Running from the car he made it to his class only two minutes late and didn't have to sit by his teacher during recess. Knute, who went to a different school than Doug and was dropped off second, was almost fifteen minutes late. But his teacher, Miss Osterhaut, was newer and not as strict as Doug's. She just told him to get "seated and settled as quickly and quietly as possible." The kids at the blackboard were working on arithmetic problems. At his desk, in his notebook, she wanted him to try and figure out as many of the answers as he could.

A pattern developed. Two or three mornings a week Doug, Knute and his mother would go to the rink and then to the restaurant for breakfast. A few times she and Doug were having such a good time skating or Mrs. Pescadoor wanted to have a more leisurely breakfast, so they agreed to employ the doctor's appointment ruse again. Mostly though they'd just about keep to their schedule; Doug would get to school approximately on time, Knute would be about fifteen minutes late.

And all members of the group were at least content. In Knute's case, as I have suggested before, his life did not yet include many things that *he* had decided to do. Getting out of bed, dressing, skating, meals, school, homework, TV, undressing, bathing, sleep—one force or another had scheduled these activities for him. And in the course of doing each one he found his own sub-activities—trying to trace a question mark on the new ice, mixing the various elements of his dinner into a paste, trying to learn to write with both hands simultaneously, playing with his testicles, trying with the tip of his pencil to pin a strand of the hair of the girl sitting in front of him to the back of her chair.

Miss Osterhaut, though—she did not share the ten-year-old Knute's life goals. After about a month of Knute being occasionally tardy, one morning when he came late she didn't ask him to get seated and settled as quickly and quietly as possible. She told the rest of the class to keep working on the problems she'd put up on the blackboard, she and Knute would just be a minute. She took him out into the hall. "I think this coming late has gotten to be a bad habit, Knute," she said.

Knute was leaning against the wall, his head bowed, eyes on his sneakers.

"You heard me, Knute?" she asked.

He nodded his head.

Miss Osterhaut put her hand under his chin and lifted his head up so she could look him in the eyes. "So from now on you're going to always be on time?"

Knute tried to nod though it was difficult with the teacher's hand under his chin. "I'll try, I hope so," he said.

"What do you mean you'll try, Knute? All the other kids in the class manage to come to school on time. If you really do try there's no reason you shouldn't succeed."

Knute nodded.

"So from this day forward you're never going to be late again. Right?"

Knute nodded.

"Don't just nod, Knute. Say, 'Yes, Miss Osterhaut, I'll never be late again.' Even if it's just a formality."

"Yes, Miss Osterhaut, I'll never be late again," Knute said. And on the mornings when they went to the rink he changed out of his skates promptly and was ready with his breakfast order. He put his coat on when his mother indicated she was ready to leave the restaurant.

But of course these efforts didn't have much effect on the time he got to school. This was determined by his mother—the amount of time she lingered over her coffee, her one last cigarette . . .

A few weeks later Miss Osterhaut took him out into the hall again. "Knute Pescadoor!" she said. "This has got to stop! I can't be the nice guy anymore about this. You have got to get yourself to school on time!"

Knute was leaning against the wall, looking down at his sneakers.

"Why are you late? Can you tell me that?"

"We go skating at the new college rink."

"Before school?"

He nodded.

"Who's we?"

"We?"

"Yes, who do you go skating with?"

"My mother and this friend of ours—his name's Doug."

"Who's class is he in?"

"Who, Doug? He doesn't go to this school. He goes to Ludlow."

"And he's late to school twice a week too, or no?"

"I don't think so. We drop him off first."

"So you're late because you're the second one to get dropped off, is that it?"

Knute nodded, and he smiled, thinking the teacher had decided the arrangement was OK.

Miss Osterhaut shook her head though. "No. No. You can't be coming late, interrupting our math class two or three days a week because of ice-skating."

"I do good in math."

"You do good, you do well—you could do better. That's not the point, Knute. It's an interruption for the rest of the students, some of whom are not doing as well as you. They need the time."

Knute focused on the sworls of gray and blue in the linoleum around his sneakers.

"You have to be here on time, Knute, I'm sorry. I can't have you missing class time and interrupting the other students so you can go skating with your friend. You had better speak to your mother. Tell her she just has to get you here on time. I can't make an exception for this."

Knute spoke to his mother that afternoon when they were driving from school to the municipal rink. "My teacher is mad at me because I come late when we go to the rink in the morning," he said.

"You come late? Not really," Mrs. Pescadoor said. "I always try to get you and Doug to school on time."

"Yes, I know, but usually I'm about fifteen minutes late."

"That's not true. That can't be true. Your teacher's exaggerating . . . Maybe five minutes . . . And what's five minutes? I can't believe the teachers these days. Why don't they teach something instead of sniffling around about the rules all the time!"

Knute let the matter drop. The next morning they went skating he suggested to his mother that if they didn't hurry he was going to be late, but she said she refused to get indigestion and spoil her morning "because of some idiotic teacher's love affair with rules. Five minutes late! If that teacher dares to give you any more trouble you tell her to call me and we'll have a little talk. Or else I'm calling her and she'll find out quick that teachers don't rule the roost. At least not when it comes to people's own children!"

As it happened, Miss Osterhaut did the calling. And when Mrs. Pescadoor answered the phone and realized who it was she felt panicked. Now she was in trouble! She hadn't gotten Knute to school on time, they [a mythic they] were going to be angry with her. They *were* angry with her. "Good morning, Miss Osterhaut," she said. "How are you doing? How is Knute doing? I hope he isn't in any trouble."

Miss Osterhaut was quite nervous herself. The year before, her first year as a teacher, she'd had to call a parent about an incontinent child. The father had gotten on the phone and yelled at her, cussed. Now she answered Mrs. Pescadoor, "No, no, he's fine, everything's fine."

"I'm relieved to hear everything's fine," Mrs. Pescadoor said.

"Me too, but—But—"

"Oh, are you calling 'cause he was late a couple times last month? It's all my fault, it's not his fault. I try to get him to school on time."

"Yes, I know—The problem is—The fact is, Knute—"

"It won't happen anymore."

"That's good to hear."

"No, really. If I were you I wouldn't worry about it. I don't know what we'll have to do, but whatever it takes—we'll do it! We'll never be late again. How's that?"

"That's good to hear. And I'll appreciate it, and I think Knute will too. First period we do our math. I know he has a lot of natural ability in math, but still, in the long run, he's missing something, by coming late as often as he has been."

"I know. That's why I'm telling you it has to stop. And if it has to stop, it will stop. You have my word of honor."

"Fine. That's very good."

Except phrases like "you have my word of honor" come and go with Mrs. Pescadoor. They sound good to her when she says them. And, basically, that's enough for her. She can go back to her business, without confusing her life with whatever it is she has promised she is going to do.

She tried a few times at the restaurant not asking for a hot top on her coffee, doing the crossword puzzle but not the a-crostic, but—Well, for instance, one thing she told herself was that one reason she was sometimes a little late places was just because she never knew what the exact time was.

And there was some truth in this. Knute's mother has an antique, carved wood grandfather's clock in her front hall, a cuckoo clock in her upstairs hall, and often two or three watches under the seat of her station wagon waiting for her to take them to the jeweler to be repaired or to remember where she left them. She likes wearing a watch. But the times all her watches and clocks show only occasionally happen to be correct. And she has never gotten in the habit of looking at watches or clocks as a way of finding out the time.

It is equally true that, by the time Knute reached the fourth grade, Mrs. Pescadoor had been having at least two cups of coffee with breakfast every morning for more than twenty years. She didn't feel fully awake, alive, ready to enjoy her day without both of those cups. And she didn't like the idea of having to rush through the morning paper. Rushing—she couldn't see the point of it. Nor could she really do it.

This frustrated Miss Osterhaut greatly. It got beyond the simple issue of whether Knute was in class on time. Control— if a student kept coming late and she couldn't do anything about it, could she maintain the necessary discipline in other areas, particularly with this one student, but also with the other students? Could she be effective in making sure the other students got to school on time? No, she believed. A statistical survey would have contradicted her findings, but nonetheless she noticed more and more of her students coming a few minutes late. She knew why too: They had seen Knute get away with it.

She wasn't big on discipline or punishment; what she most liked about teaching were the actual subjects, and getting kids to, at least occasionally, forget about their hair or their baseball, who their friends were, television. To wonder instead about the past, or how people in other cultures lived, what other kinds of children might enjoy or worry about.

Nonetheless she believed that without discipline this teaching couldn't take place. She'd been taught this in college and had observed it as an assistant and when teaching the year before. Once kids started getting out of control they very quickly progressed to completely out of control. Which meant at least a week of yelling and punishments before she could get back to teaching any subjects. To say nothing of being able to relax after school.

Yet—what could she do? Knute would come in late, two or three times a week. She tried taking him out in the hall and talking to him again, but he just said—correctly, she somehow felt—that he didn't know what he could do. He was always ready, but he had to get a ride from his mother. Did he have to go skating? The days he didn't go skating he seemed usually to be on time. Because those days he could walk from his house, he said. And he said he could ask his mother about not going skating. He didn't know what she would say.

His mother said it was ridiculous that the three of them should give up the skating which they all enjoyed so much just because Knute's teacher had a bug in her ear about a couple minutes of maybe being late. And when Miss Osterhaut called her again she was again very apologetic. She explained to her about her problems with clocks, watches and the time, and promised to be a "good soldier" from that moment on. Which of course turned out not to have anything to do with getting Knute to school by eight.

Finally Miss Osterhaut went to the assistant principal. She hadn't wanted to do this. She didn't particularly like the assistant principal or his approach to disciplining children. Also she was a new teacher, with a short contract. She didn't think it was good to be bringing problems to one of her bosses. But some of her fellow teachers urged her to. This is exactly the kind of situation the assistant principal is here to deal with, they said, and (disingenuously) they assured her that they frequently brought similar problems to him.

Mr. Linsman, the assistant principal, arranged for a conference in his office one day after school. With, as he put it, "the mother, the child, the teacher and myself." The atmosphere was more juvenile court hearing than, say, informal chat. Mr. Linsman sat behind his desk on his rolling office chair, the other three participants in straight-backed wooden chairs in front of him. He asked each of them to give his or her side of the story. As they did this he leaned back, his arms folded across his chest, head tilted, forehead wrinkled as if with concern or thought. After Knute, the last to speak, had given his explanation—he didn't want to be late, it just always happened that way he guessed; he tried always to be ready—Mr. Linsman got up and came around to the front of his desk, then leaned back, his buttocks pressing against the top edge of the desk. "Let me put it to you very simply, Mrs. Pescadoor. And Knute—because this is your responsibility even more than your mother's. Your child, you—Knute—must be in school on time every day unless there is a valid, most probably it would be a medical, excuse. This is the law. That does not mean if you bring your child late to school—even every day of the week for a month—you're going to end up in court or in jail. What the law says and what can practically be done are not the same things.

"But. That is not to say we are going to sit back and let you come late, let you interrupt Miss Osterhaut's class and the problems I know she prepares very carefully in order to teach her students the material they have to learn. Miss Osterhaut has said you do very well in math; that is good to hear and it is nice of her to say that under the circumstances. But, there are twenty-seven other students in that classroom. For some of them mathematics does not come so easily.

"So. I'm putting it to you very simply. From now on, Mondays through Fridays at 8:00 A.M. sharp I will be at Miss Osterhaut's door. If you, Knute, are in the classroom by then— fine. If not, I'll be there when you arrive. And when you arrive I'll bring you here to my office. I've got plenty of old arithmetic workbooks. You can work in one of them until the math class is over. Then I'll take you down to your classroom and you can rejoin your fellow students. Either way we won't have you interrupting Miss Osterhaut anymore. Is that clear?"

Knute nodded wearily. What could he do? The whole thing was just mixed up. It was up to his mother what time he got to school. And he didn't see any reason for Miss Osterhaut and Mr. Linsman to be taking the time he got to school so personally.

Mr. Linsman wanted him to say out loud that he understood what the arrangement would be. Sure, "Yes," he said, he understood what the arrangement would be. His mother said she understood it and would do everything in her power to make sure he was at school and in Miss Osterhaut's class on time "come hell or high water." Mr. Linsman said that was good, and Miss Osterhaut nodded and said she wasn't worried about hell or high water but she did sincerely hope the problem was behind them.

After they were by themselves Knute again suggested to his mother they give up on the skating, or at least take a break, wait until Mr. Linsman had stopped waiting for him. But his mother said no, that wasn't necessary. She was going to have him in school on time from now on. It wasn't fair to him, making him miss part of his class. It was her fault. But she had the situation under control. Here was her plan: Instead of stopping skating at 7:00, they'd stop at 6:50. Of course it was terrible that they had to lose those ten minutes of skating on account of the ridiculous education system in their town, but if that was the way it had to be, that was the way it had to be.

Knute said he didn't know. "Maybe we're going to have to stop going skating before school. You know, I think Mom, in a way that is what's going to happen."

Mrs. Pescadoor said he didn't really mean that, he was just afraid of Mr. Linsman. She understood. He was a mean person, very strict, too strict. But Knute didn't have to worry because he had her, his mother. No matter what that Mr. Linsman did she would always be there waiting for him after school to take care of him and cheer him up. And besides! Mr. Linsman wasn't going to do anything because from now on they were going to be in school on time.

No. Not merely on time. They were going to be at that school so early Knute would have to go find the janitor to let him into the school building! Or they'd drive to the teachers' parking lot and wait in the car until *Mr. Linsman* showed up. And if he wasn't there by 7:30, or whenever he was supposed to be there—they'd throw him into the back of their car and drive him to their house and make *him* do the arithmetic problems.

As Knute's mother saw it, part of what she did for her son was keep his spirits up—get him to laugh, keep him from disappearing into his private games, his silence. She did not see how much she had encouraged this aspect of his personality, but she did recognize that he had had a certain withdrawn quality since birth. Her two other children—Well, Nick Jr., Knute's older brother, was certainly not bashful about stating his needs or opinions; and you couldn't have more energy than Anne, Knute's older sister.

The year after the lateness controversy, one day during lunch at school, Knute got in a food fight that turned into a fistfight. Mr. Linsman called Mrs. Pescadoor to come take Knute home for the rest of the day. When she arrived, and Mr. Linsman began giving her his speech for the parents of children who'd gotten in trouble, she pulled Knute's jacket back and down over his arms the way she'd seen TV policemen do with suspects. She kicked Knute's leg lightly on the back of the knee so his leg buckled. She picked him up, told Mr. Linsman she had to go "take care of him." Carried him out of the school, down the steps and into the car, and burnt rubber speeding away. She drove out onto the interstate, told Knute she had to get him across the state line before nightfall when the dogs would be out. She said she had decided Mr. Linsman was "the most pompous bozo this side of the Mississippi," and as far as she was concerned if he said Knute had done something wrong, that probably meant he'd done something right.

Back when Knute was in the fourth grade, the evening after the meeting with Mr. Linsman and Miss Osterhaut, Knute's mother chattered away, putting Mr. Linsman down, making up jokes: Why did Mr. Linsman always walk around with his hands in the back of his pockets? To hold the hair across his ass. Et cetera. She took Knute to the store to get a big T-bone steak, baking potatoes, sour cream and chocolate chip ice cream—"everything for a perfect dinner—just for you and me."

These efforts did not impress Knute as much as one might assume. For one, steak, potatoes with sour cream and choco-late chip ice cream were not Knute's favorite foods but his mother's. And, his father owned and operated three restaurants and was rarely home before eleven; his brother was at college; and his sister, who was in high school, kept her own hours and had her own diet. Those days it was almost always just Knute and his mother for dinner.

Nonetheless, Knute recognized that in her own way his mother was trying to cheer him up. Which deepened his sense of the absurdity of the whole affair and the futility of his trying to do anything about it. In his view, Miss Osterhaut, Mr. Lins-man and his mother were engaged in a battle, and he was the innocent bystander—so why did he need cheering up?

The next morning, at 5:30, when his alarm rang for skating, he got out of bed, walked into the bathroom and was sick in the sink. He went to his parents' room and whispered to his mother that he was too sick to skate or go to school. He got the portable television and the guide to the week's programs down from his mother's bureau and took them back to his room. Closed his door, set the machine up on a chair, turned it on and kept right on watching until he fell asleep early that evening.

The next day he woke up early, feeling fine. His mother still had the meeting and Mr. Linsman's test fresh in her mind; they skated only twenty minutes and Knute got to school early. And he was either early or on time the next few skating mornings after that.

But—as Knute understood all along—Mr. Linsman's interest in triumphing over boys was greater than his mother's ability to adjust her habits to suit her son's interests. The morning was going to come. His mother was going to sip a little more slowly on her coffee, or get in a conversation with the lady at the cash register, or want to buy a pack of cigarettes from the machine and not be able to find the change she was sure she had in her purse.

Mrs. Pescadoor loves shooting and watching home movies. Among her collection she has certain favorites. The family all gathered at a beach resort, dressed up for dinner and coming out of their hotel. Her daughter Anne sitting on a horse for the very first time. Her grandchildren (Knute's older brother's kids) playing on a slide at a motel pool in the South. She and Knute outside one of the towers of Notre Dame in Paris, the Eiffel Tower showing in the background.

As Knute has grown up he has found himself assembling his own home-movie collection, in his head. It has come to include footage of him arriving at school that one morning, knowing he was already a few minutes late, imagining that very morning Mr. Linsman had given up waiting for him to come late. Or maybe, if he could look like he really wanted to get to class as soon as possible, probably Mr. Linsman would let him into the room.

No, he decided. He had failed the test. Mr. Linsman would be taking him to his office for math problems. His hand dragging on the banister he walked slowly up the stairs, through the first set of doors, through the stairwell, the second set of doors, into the hall. He peeked to his left, and down the corridor, toward the end where Miss Osterhaut's classroom was. Sure enough, there was Mr. Linsman, hands in his back pockets, starting to walk slowly down the hall toward him. Smiling.

At first Knute too just walked slowly, eyes down, watching his sneakers move across the floor, onto or past the cracks between the tiles. Then he broke into a trot, feeling this was what he was supposed to do, make it look like he was trying.

Mr. Linsman continued walking slowly in the opposite direction, down the hall toward Knute. When about ten feet remained between the two of them, Mr. Linsman said, "Morning."

"Morning," Knute panted, his trot stuttered a moment, and then he headed to his left to make a wide circle around the administrator.

Mr. Linsman moved sideways and reached out his right arm, catching Knute around the chest. Without saying a word he turned Knute's body around so it faced the way he himself was going, down the hall to his office.

*

Knute had a good time that morning in Mr. Linsman's office. He liked doing math problems, particularly in workbooks such as the one the assistant principal gave him. In which the problems weren't interrupted by instructions, teaching. There were just numbers, page after page of numbers and symbols for arithmetic operations and lines under which he was to write in more numbers, answers.

The small desk Mr. Linsman had him sit at was so positioned that two feet in front of Knute and on his right side were blank, not particularly clean, pale yellow walls. Sitting at that desk, other people, or Knute at other times, might have felt uncomfortable, forced against those walls. On this morning, though, he enjoyed feeling pressed in there, only his back exposed to the world of sound, movement, rules and opinions.

He worked away, at no great speed, just steadily. Problem after problem. Maybe ten seconds of thought, a few marks with his pencil under a line in the workbook. Five, ten, fifteen more seconds of thought, more marks under the next line to the right. Over one more then back to the left side. Down the page, over to the next page. Turn the page and start at the top left again.

Temporarily he forgot about skating, coming late, his mother, Miss Osterhaut and Mr. Linsman. Later that morning, after Knute and Toni got in their accident, Mr. Linsman came out on the playground, took Knute by the collar and dragged him back to his office. He shouted at Knute as they went, telling him he was an "unpleasant, undisciplined wise-ass" and other, similar things. Caught up in the pleasure of self-expression, Mr. Linsman stopped in the hallway and threw Knute against the tile wall several times. Not as hard as he might have, but convincingly enough that Knute started to cry, first in front of Mr. Linsman there in the hallway, and then later, that night in his bathroom, peering into the mirror on the door, discerning faint and conjuring up large, dark, purplish marks on his shoulder blades.

But, in the early morning, as Knute sat in the office doing arithmetic problems, there was no vicious assistant principal. There was just another person, another male; a soft-spoken, older male who, like him, was working steadily—making telephone calls, opening and closing file-cabinet drawers, occasionally stepping out of the office, returning.

When the first period was over this older male told Knute he was impressed with the "diligence and application" he had shown. Said it was unusual for a boy his age, certainly for the sort of boys he usually had working at that table in his office. Then he checked Knute's answers against the teacher's manual for Knute's workbook and found only two errors. Knute could see in his face that this really surprised and impressed him. And when Mr. Linsman took him back to his classroom he put his arm around him, told him he had a great future ahead of him if only he could learn to follow the rules a little more carefully and mind his teachers better.

The assistant principal had put his arm around him, complimented him—Knute couldn't help feeling proud of himself, and special. He was grinning as he entered his classroom and found his way to his seat. For the next period he played the model student. Sat up straight in his chair. Listened carefully to every word Miss Osterhaut said about how the Indians had already been in North America before the first European settlers had gotten there, and how they had helped those settlers get adjusted to and survive their first years of North American life. As usual Miss Osterhaut mixed her explanations with questions: Can anyone in the class remember what the Massachusetts Indians showed the Pilgrims about growing corn? The fish heads, Carl? Et cetera. Knute did not wave or even smile to any of his friends in the class. He came up with responses to all Miss Osterhaut's questions and didn't blurt out what he had to say. Instead he calmly raised his hand, waited for Miss Osterhaut to call on him.

During recess most of Knute's male classmates went to play kickball on a section of the playground that had bases and a pitching rubber painted in yellow on the black asphalt. Knute went along with them. And so did a group of five of his female classmates interested in watching and/or making trouble.

The girls' leader was one Sandra, a large, broad-shouldered girl with raven black hair. In Knute's movie she has a large horse's face and spends much of her on-screen time just up the first base line along the fence, her body seemingly cast like a statue, in an awkward pose. Head and shoulders far forward, her left foot far ahead of her right. The adult Knute has at times wondered why she doesn't have her hands on her left knee, to provide the seemingly essential support and balance. Instead her arms hang down at her sides, her big hands almost touch the ground.

"Knute got pun-ished, Knute got pun-ished." On the playground, in the fourth grade, Sandra began the chant and the other girls, standing beside and in back of her along the fence, picked it up. "Knute got pun-ished, Knute got pun-ished." Over and over. In a sing-song rhythm, the accent on the "pun." A chorus of five young girls—the sound a little like a tree saw pulled back and forth—or a swing—"Knute got *pun*-ished, Knute got *pun*-ished."

The chanting began when Knute went up to the plate. When describing these events Knute labels this his "first mistake"— going up there to kick. Putting himself center stage. His "second mistake" was not just kicking the first ball the pitcher rolled to him—and then getting the hell out of there. Instead he let that first one go by. Let a couple others go by, waiting for the perfect ball that he was going to kick so far the girls were going to melt into the asphalt.

"Knute got *pun*-ished, Knute got *pun*-ished." In the thin air of a late winter morning. A thin, blue-white sky above. "Knute got *pun*-ished, Knute got *pun*-ished." Almost like a lullaby. Something you could fall asleep to, sitting with your legs extended, over against the wall of the school in the warm sun. Sounds of other children on other parts of the playground. Teachers calling to them: "Zip up your coat, Janet." "Only one on the swing at a time, Geoff and Tom." Plus these five nice girls over by the fence where the boys were playing ball. Having such a good time. Perhaps they'd come from singing class and it was one of the songs they'd just learned that they were now practicing. "Knute got *pun*-ished, Knute got *pun*-ished."

The red rubber ball rolled by Knute on the first base side. As the first step in retrieving it, he turned toward the girls. "Knute!" "Ah, nah!" "Knute! No!" They all began shrieking. "No!" "Knute!" "Knute!" "No!" "Please, Knute!" "No, please!" "Don't, Knute!"

The ball came to a stop in the middle of the group of girls' legs. He walked slowly toward it, head down, trying not to let the girls think he was even hearing, let alone being distracted or bothered by their chanting and shrieking.

"Knute, no!" "Knute, please!" The girls continued nonetheless. "Ah, no, no—*no*, Knute, please!" "Don't please, Knute."

He looked down at his hands, wondering if perhaps he was holding something in them, a baseball bat or other large, hard object, with which perhaps the girls were thinking he was threatening them.

Or maybe it was an expression on his face. But—this often frustrated him—only when he was alone in front of a mirror was he ever sure of the expression on his face.

Sandra kicked the ball the length of the playground and into the mud. And first she and then all the girls started running in the direction the ball had gone.

Knute ran after them. Dutifully playing the boy's part in a

girls' game that needed one overwrought boy to run after the girls while they shrieked and ran in front. Not aware that he was playing a part. Feeling helpless, hopeless. Nevertheless running after the girls.

For four of the girls, the idea was to run a little ways at a moderate speed; then, as Knute got close, they shrieked even more vigorously, pulled off to the side, covered their heads with their hands and crouched down, and waited excitedly to be caught, while screaming, "No, Knute! Knute, don't touch me!" Et cetera.

But Knute didn't recognize or understand this new stage of the game. As, one by one, the first four girls pulled off and stopped, panting and shrieking for him, he just kept on running. Following the girls who remained in front of him. Who quickly became just one girl—Toni.

*

Toni was a gifted runner; in high school she was a state champion; when she was Knute's elementary school classmate she consistently won the gym class races, recorded the lowest times. In telling the story of how Knute came to break her arm that morning we could set aside his frustration and say he had been challenged, he had wanted to see if he could catch Toni.

She had run to the end of the playground, where the red rubber ball had rolled. Then, instead of continuing to follow the ball's course and running through the mud there, she had turned sharply at the end of the fence and headed up the hill,

38

into the little park that surrounded the back of the school. When she had gotten to the top she had taken a right, running almost directly away from the school, into the most wooded area of the park. It had been sport to her. Running was what she liked better than anything else. She liked the motions, the wind, the warmth—and she liked speeding ahead, leading, outlasting other kids.

When she had gotten to the far corner of the park she had ducked under the large hedges and stepped out onto the sidewalk of the little residential street. She had stopped momentarily to look back at Knute, making sure he knew which hedges were the easy ones to duck between, making sure he was going to keep trying to catch her. This seeming to be the case, she had picked up the pace again, heading up the sidewalk, still further away from the school.

Another right, down the hill, back along one side of the park. Along a dirt path, into the teacher's parking lot, across the parking circle in front of the school. Toni had made a long course: When the race ended they had run more than a mile.

After passing the school she had gone down the hill even further, toward the far corner of the park. Knute could not run as smoothly as she could, his lungs ached, going downhill his thighs felt too stretched, going uphill they felt leaden. But he had long legs for his age and he was able to cover a good bit of ground with each stride. He would have liked to catch up to Toni; he managed to stay about five yards back.

She had run past and around the two tennis courts. Up again on a very uneven sidewalk, the cement squares jutting up in different directions. More trees, a traffic light off to the left and above. The fourth and final corner of the park. Where Toni (feeling the course was complete) headed to the right, across the hill, through a small grove, back toward the playground.

As she and Knute had come out of the grove and onto the top of the hill their classmates and the other kids in the school who were down on the playground gathered and moved toward the fence nearest them. They looked up and shouted. The girls generally: "Come on, Toni," and other such things. The boys: "Go, Knute . . ."

Toni and Knute both went as fast as they could. Under normal circumstances the result would have been an easy finish for her. Responding to the crowd, sensing the finish, she would have accelerated to a pace that Knute's physical gifts would not have been able to sustain. Defeat assured, Knute would have lost his desire and energy. He would have slowed to a jog, his head sagging, his eyes again fixing on the ground. He would have started telling himself how he needed better sneakers if he was going to be a runner, or maybe he'd better switch elementary schools, or at least slip up the hill and go home, get some rest.

But, on this morning, when Knute's increasingly hazy sense of Toni's bare calves, her ponytail and white sneakers began to pull away from him, he ran faster, stretched his stride out longer. He managed to close the gap. To less than a yard.

A few moments later, when he and Toni were going down the final slope and she again accelerated, and he knew she was about to have her inevitable victory, leave him with his inevitable defeat—he threw himself toward her. Head first down the hill.

His left shoulder found her lower back. She started to fall, on the slope of the hill, seeing no solid land beneath her. She put her right arm out straight. It found land. Her weight flowed down through her shoulder into her elbow and the bones of her forearm. Knute's weight followed. Then the sound of bone cracking, the sight of part of the broken end pushing against the skin.

Chapter 2

Knute's ancestors on his mother's side came to the U.S. from northern Europe during the fifty or sixty years preceding the Civil War. Their destinations weren't so much a symbolic America—land of opportunity, of religious freedom— as they were specific towns in the middle of the continent, places where they'd heard good farmland could be purchased cheaply, or where they had relatives or other members of their congregations waiting for them. At first they worked as farmers and in related trades, milling, blacksmithing, tanning. Some members of the succeeding generations stuck with farming or skilled labor; many became merchants, keeping hardware, grain and dry goods stores, or selling farm equipment. By the twentieth century some had moved to the capital of their state; some had become insurance salesmen, dentists, pharmacists.

Unlike many American blacks, Irish and Jews, these Midwesterners had not been forced to emigrate; they do not maintain a sense of a painful or difficult separation or resettling, or of continuing alienation from their Old World cultures. Many of the immigrants had been motivated by the desire to live and raise their children in small communities of people who shared their brand of Christianity. By the time Knute was born, the families had been doing this for a hundred years; their interest in God and concern over interpretations of the Gospel had waned; their preference for living in small communities with people like them had persisted. Almost all the immigrants had sought to escape conflicts, poverty and disease in their European worlds. They had thought that given a chance to do things their way, far from lazy, confused, corrupt or domineering members of their race, they would be able to make their own peaceful, secure, reasonably prosperous world. And, more or less, and only temporarily, they had.

Their descendants have resolved to let bygones be bygones. Anger, religious ardor; risking one's life, or one's savings, to emigrate to another country; being poor, peasants—yes, probably relatives of theirs have felt, done or been such things. But, the descendants have decided it wouldn't be appropriate to dwell on all this. They themselves were born to middle-class American parents; as their children were, and as they expect their grandchildren will be.

The past, their history? Well, some of the men read narratives and biographies—for instance, of LaSalle, the building of the Panama Canal, the Lewis and Clark expedition, Theodore Roosevelt. To visitors and newcomers, most of them, men and women, will note that their families have been in the state, or in certain towns, awhile, since as long as any of them

43

can remember. Perhaps an ancestor helped build a certain church or grange or is buried in a certain cemetery.

In the more distant past?

Well, what can they remember from history class in school? John Smith and Pocahontas. The Boston Tea Party and Paul Revere spreading the news that the Redcoats were coming. One if by land, two if by sea. Or was it the other way around? Davy Crockett and Dan'l Boone. Moving west in covered wagons, banding together for protection from the Indians. Abraham Lincoln splitting rails. The Gettysburg Address— once, back in school, they had been able to recite every word.

In the twentieth century some of the women in the families, generally in old or late middle age, have taken up genealogy. They are to some degree curious about who their ancestors actually were, but mainly it is a diversion, a hobby. They have raised their children, and they don't have to or want to take jobs. Some don't care for golf, gardening, knitting, preserving. Some like all those activities and just feel the need for one more, something a little more intellectual.

They have joined immigrant and antiquarian societies, received magazines, corresponded with members of their or other societies in other parts of the U.S. and in Europe. They have written to and a few of them have visited Europeans who, according to the Americans' reading and calculations, are their distant relatives. They have had calligraphers write out their family trees, which generally, somewhere around the fifteenth or sixteenth century, link up with a noble lineage and head on back with it to Chief Rollo, King Canute, or one or more Holy

Roman emperors. These women are not skeptics; they believe what their trees tell them, that they have noble blood. They have had copies of their ancestors' coats-of-arms framed, and they have hung these next to the trees, over the mantel in the living room, in the front hall, or behind the bar in their basement dens.

A few of the more energetic and scholarly of the women have gone a step further and tried to determine if any of the lesser names on their trees (that is, their more direct relatives) played roles in established history. Perhaps one was a captain of an artillery company in a famous battle, or a minister who wrote an early Protestant tract. Of greater interest are artifacts—a copy of that hypothetical tract or one of the captain's letters home to his young bride, or a grain sack from an ancestor's mill.

The work of these more energetic researchers has made a bit of an impression on Knute. When he was eight he and his mother brought home from his grandparents' summer cabin three clay jars that his grandfather had on a shelf in his workshop next to his pipe wrenches. His grandfather said his sister-in-law bought them on a trip to Germany and told him they had been manufactured in a certain religious community to which one of his family's ancestors had belonged. According to the date written into the bottoms, the jars were almost 200 years old.

Knute went with his mother to take the jars to the city to be appraised by an antique dealer. His mother was a little disappointed by the quote of $100. But they took the pots back home, and, to the right of the fireplace in the living room, they cleared the top shelf for them. This enhanced their stature. All the other shelves on either side of the fireplace were almost always filled with piles of magazines, picture puzzles, games, socks, decks of cards, the shawls and blankets he, his mother and sister would cover themselves with when napping on the living room sofa, or stretching out to read, watch TV . . . But on this one high shelf there would just be the three jars, evenly spaced, the largest on the left, mid-size in the middle, smallest on the right.

Throughout his childhood, coming into the living room of his parents' first home, and then later, in the living room of the second home, Knute would stop in the middle of the rug, look up at these jars. Plain, and now empty, objects that, apparently, had to stand in for half of his history. They had been purchased on another continent, from people who spoke another language. People with strong religious beliefs.

Perhaps from these people he was inheriting determination, a sense of purpose. A desire to break precious pottery? He saw himself in this historic community. He in his contemporary clothing, on his bike perhaps. The citizenry dressed up in starched linens and clogs, spinning and hammering at the forge and seated on stools milking like the actors at a tourist re-creation of such a village.

When he was twelve years old, outside the church after his grandfather's funeral service, Knute was approached by an old lady who, as an adult, he remembers with black netting hanging in front of a knobby-cheeked, smiling face; a royal blue pillbox hat. She introduced herself as one of his grandmother's first cousins, and the only other thing he remembers about her is her telling him how she had recently read a "long and lovely poem about a handsome Welsh prince from back in the days of King Arthur." He had one of the family names, and the family did have a little Welsh blood. So, quite possibly, the model for the poem, the real-life prince, was one of their ancient ancestors. In the poem, she said—her eyes lighting up—the prince's symbol was the griffin.

It seemed to indicate or suggest something. By the time Knute was in his late twenties he was sure there was meaning, significance there. A Welsh prince. A griffin. The head and wings of an eagle, body and tail of a lion.

So? So, what?

Knute's mother's father, "Grandpa A" (for Anson, his surname), had run a paint and wallpaper store that had been established by Knute's grandmother's father. As far back as Knute could remember though, Grandpa A had been retired. He spent almost the entire warm season from May through October at the lakeside cabin, and during the winter he and Knute's grandmother took trips to visit their children and grandchildren, such as Knute and his mother, who lived outside the state. The store was run by Margaret, Knute's mother's older sister, and her husband Bob, and they were making monthly payments to Grandpa A to buy it from him.

Out at the cabin summers, or when relatives came to visit, one portion of the adult conversation Knute overheard concerned this store. At the cabin, on Sundays when Margaret and Bob would come out, the lunch conversation would often be dominated by Margaret's excited descriptions of their projects.

For almost fifty years the store had been in the same downtown location. By the time Margaret and Bob took over, many of the neighboring stores had moved to suburban malls, other businesses had closed. A series of cheap, unattractive and low-income housing projects had been built, starting just two blocks away. Some gentle lobbying by Knute's grandfather notwithstanding, the road the store was on had not been re-paved in years and parts of the surface had worn through to the dirt. Trees had died and had not been replaced.

As over time the lunch conversations revealed, Margaret and Bob first looked for a new location; then they found an ideal one—except it was just an empty lot—on the main street of one of the wealthiest suburbs. They decided to buy the lot and build a new store—from scratch! Bob's brother was going to lend them the money. Then they got a great young architect to agree to design the place. And this architect was very much in demand in the northern suburbs then. There were the plans to go over, descriptions of how the building was progressing. Moving out of the old place; the grand opening. Then, the next project was entering into cooperative agreements with interior decorators. And so on.

For his part, Grandpa A was not a big talker. Margaret would go on about how she was moving the store, looking for a buyer for the building in which he had worked for forty years. She'd give her opinions as to what had been wrong with the way the store had been operated previously, and Bob, who had studied business in college, would provide some data or theory to reinforce Margaret's statements. Knute's grandfather wouldn't say anything. He'd lean forward on his elbows on his end of the table, his fingers twiddling the salt shaker or his teaspoon. Only half listening. Periodically telling himself, it's their store now. They should do what they want with it. God knows I didn't have any original ideas about how to run a business.

Occasionally, when Knute and his mother were out fishing with his grandfather, or working with him, say splitting firewood and bringing it into the house, he would look up and make a comment, or he'd ask them a question: "They do have a lot of ideas and enthusiasm, don't they—Margaret and Bob?" "It seems like they both have their heads on their shoulders, Margaret and Bob—don't you think?" "Do you think they help, those business courses Bob took?" "Do you think I'm charging the right amount for the store? I don't want them to feel extra pressure on account of the debt. But I think the family as a whole should get something for the business."

Knute's mother would fire off her opinions, letting her father have the satisfaction of hearing spoken all he didn't want to and couldn't say himself: "Margaret thinks she's the first person ever to own a paint and wallpaper store. . . . By God, you'd think they'd at least ask your advice, Dad, before they decided to move your store! The suburbs, the suburbs, the suburbs—she makes it sound like God himself has moved to the suburbs—and He's gonna repaint His house every year, right? Let them pay you *twice* what they're paying, that's what I say. If they're such with-it, on-the-ball business-ers, they can afford it."

When his grandfather would turn to him and ask him what he thought, Knute would shrug. Say something like "I liked

49

the old store." Which he had. It had been simple. Big picture windows in front, alternating black and aquamarine tiles on the floor. Metal shelves to the ceiling, filled with cans of paint. And in back there had been more and higher shelves. Way up above his head, columns of paint cans. Long aisles, the pallor of fluorescent light. While his mother helped out on the floor or at the register, he would wander up and down those aisles, stretch out his arms and slalom from side to side, his fingertips flicking the fronts of the cans.

*

On the other side of Knute's family, history began with his father's father, in his late teens, getting on a bicycle in his fishing village in southern Italy, and heading for the nearest large port. From there he had taken a boat to America. He'd gone to live with his mother's sister's family in an eastern city, had been given work on the wharves, unloading, cleaning, packing and loading fish. He did such jobs for the next thirty-five years, or until he had bad arthritis and adult children, particularly Knute's father, to help support him. Then he went to work as a bank guard.

Knute's father's mother was sent to him. After Knute's grandfather had been in the United States a few years he went to the apartment of a middle-aged Italian woman and gave her a sum of money that was roughly equal to all his savings. Almost a year later, one morning the foreman called him off his job, he was to go back to the lady's apartment. There he was presented with the woman who he had the pleasure of spending the rest of his life with.

This was "Grandpa P's" slightly overdramatic way of relating the story; in fact he had known the woman, or girl, almost since birth. She was from his town and only a few years younger than him. They hadn't been teenage lovers or even particularly noticed one another when they were growing up. The marriage *had* been arranged, by this woman in the U.S., a man in their town and their parents. But, when they'd been told the news, they'd recognized one another's names. Meeting in the lady's apartment they'd recognized one another's faces.

Throughout his youth Knute was fascinated by this story of his grandparents' arranged marriage. In certain moods when he was in his late teens and early twenties it would slip into his mind—his grandmother having to give this man sex, cook for him, do his laundry for her whole life, just because he paid for her to come to America. He tried to imagine the moment of their meeting. A small, dark apartment; all the shades drawn; smells of Italian food—garlic, oregano. Rosa, his grandmother, had died before Knute was born; still he could make parts of a her out—someone smaller even than his grandfather; looking up at him; long black hair pulled back in a ponytail. She'd been rushed—in a big black car, the fantasy was—from the dock, through crowded city streets to the apartment. She didn't know a word of English. She felt impossibly far from the fishing boats pulled up on the sand, the ripples of moonlight on the water that Knute imagined for her Italian village.

His grandfather lived into his nineties, until Knute was thirteen. Knute saw him fairly often, including the one or two times a year when Knute's father would fly him out to the Midwest to spend a few weeks. One afternoon during one of the last of these visits, Knute's grandfather talked to him at length about his first years in America, the "first American Mrs. Pescadoor." His grandfather told him that when she was young Rosa was extremely beautiful, short, with a cute little belly and rear end, little round cheeks too. It was he who planted in Knute's head the idea of Rosa's alienation and innocence. He said for years she hardly understood anything that was going on around her even if it was in Italian. She didn't understand cities or the ways people in them will act. He used to send her to the vegetable market with a couple dollars and a list of things to buy for soup. She'd come back completely broke with the two sorriest onions in America. Sometimes crying as well: She used to get very frustrated because she thought she was no good as a wife; she would go out the apartment door repeating out loud to herself that this time she wasn't going to get cheated, and still would end up having spent all the money and having so much less than all the other women.

Knute's grandfather told him he didn't care. He'd just laugh at Rosa, try to cheer her up, go out with her again and try and recover some of his money or vegetables.

Before Rosa came he was very lonely, he said. He had lived with relatives and they had been very nice to him, treated him like their son, but . . . Something was missing. Rosa and him had made a home. In that same apartment with his relatives. But it had been different. They'd gotten their own little stove. She had sewn curtains for their room, white with big red polka dots.

He remembered their first Saturday nights. For years and years, he said, his schedule had been to work every night except Saturday, starting his week at midnight Sunday night, finishing around nine or ten the next Saturday morning. After Knute's father reached school-age and some of the other kids started coming along, Rosa was very busy with them and had to keep their schedule. And often too she helped a woman in the neighborhood who took in laundry. Or, when the family was really short of money she'd go to work as an assembler in a factory. They all worked too hard. He, Knute's grandfather, used to see his family only in the mornings, before he went to bed, and then again for dinner until he had to go back to work. Even Saturday nights, by midnight Rosa would be too tired to stay up with him.

But those first couple years. They were both on the same schedule. Saturday nights they'd go to this dance hall where all their friends went, or they'd just stroll with the rest of the crowd, have coffees and pastry somewhere. And then it would be midnight and they'd be wide awake and he wouldn't have to go to work. That was when they were closest and most in love. And afterward they'd sit up in bed, listening to the radio. And when it got to be close to dawn they'd sneak out of the apartment and walk over to the little park with an old fort in it that was right on the water. They had a favorite bench there.

They'd sit, maybe Rosa would have brought some fruit, and they'd watch the sun coming up over the water. All the little islands, boats.

*

Knute's parents met in the Midwest. In the large, industrial city of which the town Knute grew up in was a suburb. Knute's mother moved to this city following her sister Bridget and Bridget's husband, Michael. Michael had wanted to make a home separate from his and his wife's families, in another city, just him, his wife and the children they were going to have. About a year after they moved Bridget invited Ginny— Knute's mother—to come live with them. In jest at the city and herself, Mrs. Pescadoor used to tell Knute and his sister Anne that she'd taken her sister up on the invitation because she wanted to "see the world." At home she had been working as a nurse; she found nursing work at a hospital in her new city.

Knute's father came via the Second World War. Shortly after the war began he had enlisted in the Navy. He had ended up on an aircraft carrier in the Pacific, and, as he, over years, has passed the information on to his wife and children, in the beginning he had been put down in the engine room, assigned to stand around down there, watch the guys who actually knew how to maintain the engines work, maybe hand them a wrench every once in a while or get them a sandwich and coffee.

The ship had an entertainment hall, and when he was off-duty he used to hang around there, help with the decorating, the setting up. Then he had worked up a little skit/comedy act for him and two of his friends in the engine room to perform, and it seemed to have gone over pretty well; they had him and his friends up on that stage every Friday and Saturday night till the boat pulled back into San Francisco Bay and they got to go home.

Somewhere along in there, it seemed like it had been 1943, in the winter, they'd appointed him MC. And then, it wasn't more than a month or two later, the guy who'd been running the hall/in charge of the entertainment had to be taken off the ship. It could get to your nerves, being out there, nothing around but miles of water, waves, the swell, the planes going by overhead, and then the sound of some engine far away and you'd be below decks and you didn't know if it was friend or foe and he always ended up stopping whatever it was he was doing and just standing there, listening, waiting.

When the guy left they asked him to take over, order the supplies, arrange for films, entertainers, refreshments, decorations.

When Knute was growing up, one of the adults in his parents' world was a Mr. Bishop who, as Knute's mother originally explained it to him, had "done more to help your father and our family than anybody, anybody."

For some years Charley Bishop and Nick Pescadoor (Knute's father) had been business partners. Years before Knute was born, his father had decided to get out of this partnership although Mr. Bishop very much wanted it to continue. His father had employed a combination of subtle legal moves

Mr. Bishop had never understood and an aggressive lawsuit Mr. Bishop eventually lost any will to fight. By the time Knute was born, both sides were claiming the wounds had healed, the past was thankfully forgotten, everybody was friends again.

When Knute was growing up he saw Mr. Bishop off and on. He'd come out to the Pescadoors' house for dinner. Or Knute would see him at his father's restaurant in the city. Knute was curious about him, and would question his mother: "Is he taller than most people?" "Is his skin a little purple?" Mr. Bishop was 6′4″, which of course seemed very tall to a child, and genes and lack of sun and exercise had combined to give his cheeks a violet tint. Even through the summer he continued to wear his outfit: never particularly clean, red-and-white-checked wool pants; long-sleeve, light blue shirts with large, pointed collars; and never particularly clean, pale blue or rabbit-tail white V-neck sweaters. "Does he ever get hot?" Knute would ask. And, "Why does he always dress the same?"

Among the questions that, as a child, Knute, quite unconsciously, refrained from asking were, Why did his father have to dissolve the partnership? And, how was everybody now feeling about that event, and the conflicts that had surrounded it? You could imagine though that, with their answers to Knute's more mundane questions, his parents were trying to put aside the others. His father would often laugh, maybe rub Knute's head and answer with a question: "Charley can't choose his own clothing?" "You think Charley should play a little more tennis?" Knute's mother used variations on other

56

standard parental responses: "Why don't you ask Mr. Bishop?" "Jeez you ask a lot of questions, kid!"

Except for asking his own particular brand of questions, Mr. Bishop seldom spoke. Instead, you could say, he had developed his tic; steadily, every few seconds, his right eye would wink, pulling the muscles of his right cheek up and then letting them slip down again. Knute would try not to stare and would stare and, as if he were looking at fish in a tank, he would become fascinated by the movements of the right side of Mr. Bishop's face.

"Why does he always do that?" he asked his father, his mother, his sister.

"It's too bad," his father said. "It's hard to watch."

"It's a kind of disease," his mother said.

"Just try not to think about it," Anne said.

Sometimes after seeing Mr. Bishop, Knute would announce to his mother either that he wasn't sure he liked Mr. Bishop or that he'd decided he did like him.

Mr. Bishop had been an officer on the aircraft carrier on which Knute's father served. Later when they were partners, one of Knute's father's jokes was that on the ship he had thought Mr. Bishop had been assigned the duty of wearing his white dress uniform. To keep up the boat's image, with the dolphins, or visiting Jap kamikaze pilots. And—although this was something he'd let go out of his memory and conversation—at the time, on the ship, he had also thought Charley Bishop the most idle, useless person there. He used to come

WILLIAM WARNER

and stand below the stage when visiting entertainers were re-
hearsing or Mr. Pescadoor was getting the stage set up, lighting and microphones checked. And Mr. Bishop would never
offer to help. He'd just stand there, below the stage and always
about four feet off the edge on the right. In his white uniform;
holding his hat in both hands just below his crotch. Making
about one comment per twenty minutes: "I think it looks very
good." "You dance very well I think."

In the mornings, when Mr. Pescadoor would be in the little
office he had, having his coffee and trying to get started on the
paperwork which was a major part of his job—often Charley
Bishop would walk by. Two or three times. And then he'd stop
a few feet from the open door, as if there was something he
had decided he just had to get off his chest.

At least half the time it had been compliments. He'd told
Mr. Pescadoor he had a "knack for organization. . . . A great
way of warming up a crowd." Other times Mr. Bishop would
ask questions. Rather brusquely and annoyingly, the young
Nick Pescadoor thought, though again this did not end up in
his long-term memory.

Where had Mr. Pescadoor grown up? Had he done entertainment work before? Had he ever worked in a nightclub? "Let's
suppose you were given a blank check, and could get any en-
tertainer you wanted, any kind of decor—there would be no
question of cost—what kind of club would you open?"

Charley Bishop was—as Mr. Pescadoor had thought at the
time—just passing his mornings in the Navy with these questions and Nick Pescadoor's polite but begrudgingly short answers. But his thoughts got caught up in and drawn along by

his questions. And one morning, when the war was as good as over for all but the residents of two Japanese cities, Charley Bishop's seemingly idle comment was that his father was a very successful obstetrician in a certain Midwestern suburb. The adjacent city was prospering and was sure to do even better after the war. How would Nick like to go 50–50 with him? He'd get his father to put up the money, Nick would give his gift, his talent.

"For what?" Mr. Pescadoor asked, half excited and half even more annoyed than usual because of the temptation he sensed before him, the temptation to spend part of his life with this idle, possibly homosexual, apparently talentless man and his awkward questions.

The answer was running a nightclub, and of course Knute's father-to-be, a fish-handler's son in his early twenties, was in no position to refuse the offer—to *want* to refuse the offer, no matter how uncomfortable his prospective partner made him.

So he had come to the city. To run "The Full Moon" (formally, "Full Moon Over The Pacific"). As Charley Bishop soon began telling himself, his father and Nick, clearly Charley Bishop "knew talent when he saw it." His man Nick Pescadoor rented a space and stocked and decorated it for less than two-thirds the amount he and his father had budgeted. And Pescadoor had a knack for finding singers, dancers, comedians who were about to make it big. So the Bishops soon were able to advertise The Full Moon as *the* place in town to see future stars. Who—another of Pescadoor's talents—were being paid novice wages, staying on stage each show an extra five, ten minutes each. While the customers drank what they thought were fancy liquors but were actually the house brands that every afternoon in the basement first Nick Pescadoor himself, then Nick and Ginny Pescadoor themselves poured into the fancy bottles.

He ran the club for five years (all before Knute was born). He enjoyed running it the whole time, but after the first year much of his satisfaction was in preparing for his future. When he'd take the money he was saving—his 50 percent cut of the profits he declared, plus the cash he was skimming from the register every night—and take his share of the sale of the club, and start his own business.

As over the years the fantasy developed, and developed from a fantasy to plans, the form of this business shifted, from a nightclub to a restaurant. A family restaurant, Italian food, big portions. Less of the hassles—agents, moody entertainers, drunken customers, black market suppliers, police, protection, friends of the police or of the protection. Less of the ups and downs of fashion—having constantly to come up with new things—new stars, new routines, decor, drinks. Having to keep selling the public that he had it all, all new and hot, and packed with successful, fun-loving people.

He felt correctly that it couldn't last, he couldn't last. He had come up with one thing that happened to be working, a kind of entertainment that fit with how the local young people with money, at that time, wanted to be entertained. He had his little arrangements; his nightly dipping into the pot. All this was making it work, making it worthwhile. But it just wasn't secure. He had no wealth, and he had relatives, children who were counting on him. He needed a regular, reliable source of income.

He just hoped and he developed an ulcer at twenty-seven in part from worrying that the cracks in his operation would start showing before he'd sold out. Started opening his restaurants (the plan quickly expanded to more than one). Simple cheap food, steady turnover, families. Last seating nine o'clock. Nothing dramatic. Just the steady money of people ordering one or two drinks before dinner, beer and wine, pie à la mode for dessert.

*

Knute's mother likes to tell him and his brother and sister—particularly if their father is present—that, before she met their father, she went "only very occasionally" to The Full Moon. It was too expensive and she preferred places where the *customers* could dance. She liked to dance. But Frank, The Full Moon bartender, knew how to make a good gin fizz, he didn't try to overload you with gin. The girls certainly had nice equipment. And their father was the cutest MC in town.

So she would go along when her group of young doctors and nurses from the hospital wanted to go. Just waiting to get the chance to meet that cute MC? Certainly not, Mrs. Pescadoor likes to say. A short little Italian? Besides, she says (referring to the fact that Mr. Pescadoor is two years younger than her), it was clear just looking at him that he was under age.

Didn't Charley Bishop know there were child-labor laws? They weren't just for white people, Italians were included too. Another line is that she had her eye on an ophthalmologist.

Nevertheless. One February night. Her hospital group decided to go to The Full Moon and she'd gone along with them, as had Anne, her closest friend. Anne, who was also a nurse at the hospital, had recently gotten engaged to a pediatrics resident, John, who she had been dating for a few years. There was no question in any of their friends' minds that Anne and John would get married as scheduled, and should get married. But, with the church reserved and her dress and their rings ordered, Anne was enjoying the further luxury of wondering if she was making a mistake. Did she really love John? Was the timing right? Perhaps they both needed to sow more wild oats. Did Ginny, or whichever of their friends she happened to be talking to, realize—neither she nor John had ever *really* been in love with anyone else? Maybe one of them should go to Paris for a year, the other to Rome. They'd each have a romantic affair—become more sexually experienced—and then they could come back and get married. What did Ginny think about that!

The first time she heard Anne make this suggestion, Ginny was disturbed and confused. "I think if you love somebody, Anne," she said, "you wouldn't want to go off and find somebody else to have sex with." The second and third times Ginny got annoyed at her friend for continuing to joke around about something so serious and so dangerous. By that February night at The Full Moon—when Anne brought the idea up for the sixth or seventh time—Ginny, tired not just of that idea but of all Anne's ideas about her marriage, and of her wedding plans, and honeymoon plans, et cetera, didn't even shrug. She sipped through her straw on her gin fizz, kept her head turned to watch the show.

Her closest friend was getting married. Anne said it wasn't going to affect their friendship, they'd still have their late night, homemade hot fudge sundaes, long days at the beach, double features, good talks. Ginny was sure Anne was wrong. She was going to be on her own, staying home or going to the movies by herself. She knew she wasn't going to like this as much as having Anne to be with.

A comedian came on stage and began telling his "life story." To get from Italy to America he'd stowed away in a shoebox. He'd hardly been two minutes on the Lower East Side before he'd walked by a sign for a job—for a shoemaker. He got drafted into the Navy and spent the war polishing shoes. Now he was going to college on the GI bill. His major? Shoe-ciology.

"I need your advice, Ginny!" Anne kept on. She was sitting to Ginny's right. She put her hand on Ginny's forearm, squeezed it to try and get Ginny's attention. Ginny did look over at her, and Anne went on: "I tried to talk to John last night about my plans to go to Gabon."

"You have plans now?" Ginny asked.

"Well, sort of," Anne said. Incorrectly: She had fantasies, fantasies she'd often talked to Ginny about, and included Ginny in. They—or she alone if Ginny didn't care to go—would live in a native village, teach classes for the mothers in sanitation and nutrition, clean and bandage the children's cuts and abrasions, take their temperatures, bring them liquids when they got the mumps. Maybe they'd teach classes for the men in reading and writing English.

But John. The night before when she'd brought up the subject, he'd just said that, assuming his practice began to provide them the kind of income he thought it should be able to, they would be able to take a trip to West Africa, and he thought such a trip could prove quite broadening. But first he needed to get the practice established; they should buy a house and get a chunk of the mortgage paid off, get started on a family. "Of course I want all those things," Anne told Ginny, as she'd told her more than once before. "I *do* want a family. And I *do* think John could be a good father for the children. . . . Eventually maybe. . . . I'm only twenty-three, he's twenty-six already— I think it makes a big difference, those three years. . . . I don't know Ginny . . ."

Ginny's thoughts had drifted away. She was hearing Anne making sounds, but wasn't hearing the stresses, the separations of sounds that indicate words, phrases, ideas or questions. She wasn't following any train of thought of her own either. In a way she was just waiting. Waiting for Anne to be off to New York on her honeymoon, at which point she would—she would be forced to—get started on her Anne-less life.

As an entr'acte diversion, a mastiff dressed in black and pink lacy undergarments was sent out on the stage. The dog walked to the front edge, near the center, and stopped, her head drooping, eyes big and wet, gray-pink lips big and loose, a white crust on the edges.

Without turning her gaze from the dog, Ginny reached back and patted Anne's arm. "Anne, look," she said.

Anne looked up, took in the scene—dog in lacy under-wear—and returned to her marital concerns. "You know, sometimes I wish my parents didn't like John so much. I think that's making it hard for me to feel that I'm making my own decision. You know, in agreeing to marry John?"

"Did you see that!" Ginny interrupted.

"What, the dog? Yes, it's very cute. But I mean, agreeing to marry John—is it my decision, or my parents'? You know, sometimes—"

"Oh, look now! This is too much!"

The MC—Nick Pescadoor—had returned to the stage and the microphone, and, as if perplexed as to where this ridicu-lous dog had come from, for a few minutes he had just stood with his head cocked to the side, looking at the dog, not saying anything. Then he had searched his pockets, showing the au-dience his keys, change, his wallet—empty. In a back pocket he had finally found a, somewhat used, red handkerchief. And "now," as Ginny spoke, he was stepping over to the dog hold-ing this handkerchief out to him, as if the dog were a bull and he were an extremely fastidious and/or extremely timid torea-dor. The dog of course was not inspired by the color red; in fact she didn't move her head, she just left her eyes and mouth open, facing the crowd. Nick tried whistling at her and pre-tending to kick her in the rear; the dog didn't move. Finally he called for a stagehand to come with a leash and drag the dog off so the show could get started again. He glanced at his watch, said in a stage whisper, "Oh god, there's only another hour till curfew. I'm going to end up having to cut some of the best parts of this show."

The band started again. The chorus girls, in *their* black and pink lace, came out on stage. "You know what I asked John today at lunch?" Anne asked Ginny.

Ginny shook her head.

"I asked him if he had ever tried to imagine what having sex with me was going to be like."

"Un-huh," Ginny said.

"But Ginny! Don't you think that was quite a question for me to ask!"

"I guess," Ginny said. What had Anne said? She'd had sex with John at lunch today? That was a question?

"I think you're off in Never-Never Land," Anne said. "It's like you haven't even heard one word I've said to you!"

Ginny looked over at Anne. "Did you read that article in the paper this morning?"

"What article?" Anne was getting exasperated.

"About that college kid who works in one of these places, or maybe it's a hotel."

"That's what he does? He works either in a nightclub or in a hotel?"

"Yeah. He breaks the bottles. He doesn't start work till like two in the morning. He's got a mask and this protective suit, and he goes down in the basement and throws all the bottles at the wall. You know, so they'll be more compact for the garbage."

"Sure sounds interesting," Anne joked.

"Hey! Miss, Miss Waitress," Ginny called to one of the waitresses who was going by their table carrying a tray of dirty glasses.

The young woman came over, bent her head toward Ginny. "Can I get you something? Another round?"

66

Ginny shook her head. "I just wanted to know if you had one of those bottle-breakers. Like there was that article about in the paper this morning."

"I'm not sure what article you mean," the waitress said. "I'm not sure I saw the paper today."

"Well, it was a good article about this college kid. You should try to get a copy of it and read it. If I still have it, I'll bring it the next time we come. What nights do you work?" That night Ginny was interested in people who weren't Anne, conversations that weren't Anne's marital musings.

"I think I better get all these glasses back to the kitchen," the waitress said. "Nice talking to you."

"Wait," Ginny said, and she got up and followed the waitress as the latter wended her way between the customers and their chairs, stopped and reached to pick up glasses, beer bottles and requests for more drinks, tried to ignore if not smile at the cracks: "I'd like two milks." "Can I buy you a drink?" "Oooh! How you swing those hips, Virginia!"

"Do you have someone to break your bottles?" Ginny asked, at the waitress's back, trying to lean toward the woman's ear so she would be able to hear the question.

The waitress didn't look back, but she tried to shrug without upsetting her tray on the neighboring customer's head.

"In the paper it was a college kid who was putting himself through college that way, you know?" Ginny asked.

Another shrug. When she had gotten to the door going into the kitchen, the waitress turned and nodded with her head in the direction of the bar, "Maybe you should talk to Frank, the bartender, about this article. I think he might know more about it than I do."

Ginny did go talk to Frank. Sitting up on a stool at the corner of the bar next to where the waitresses came to place the drink orders, she had what was called there a "Full Moon," a drink made of coconut milk and Cointreau. When Frank was working near her, she talked to him, not just about the article and bottle-breakers, but about the group she always came to The Full Moon with, her best friend Anne who was getting married, her family back home; how, in the summer, she and her father liked to go fishing every morning and afternoon, and, in the winter, *sometimes* she went out ice fishing with him.

Shortly before the show ended and the lights came up, Frank agreed to ask the manager, Nick, if Ginny could stay to watch the beer and wine bottles being broken in the basement.

"I was naive," Knute's father later liked to joke. "I should have known—women and broken bottles—a bad combination."

And Knute's mother would joke, "That's our marriage for you, one broken bottle after another."

That night at The Full Moon, Anne insisted on staying with Ginny, though she also expressed her displeasure at having to stay, at staying up so late when she had an impossible number of errands to do the next morning. Nick took Ginny to the basement room where the bottles were broken. He introduced her to a fourteen-year-old black boy, the member of the kitchen staff who did the work, and the boy showed her and Nick his special trick which, when it worked, was to get three bottles into the air and then hit them with a fourth bottle, breaking the entire group. Ginny asked the boy if he would teach her, and Nick went and found her an old dishwasher's uniform, a cook's hat and some sunglasses (to protect her eyes). And she spent almost an hour down there, very happily absorbed in trying to learn—first, how to get three bottles in the air simultaneously; second, how to hit all of them with one bottle, *before* they fell; third—what took her a few more nights to master—to hit the bottles with such force they would crash against the back wall and break.

Upstairs, Anne sat down, rested her head on her arms on a table, and promptly fell asleep. Nick worked near her, adding up the receipts and updating his books. When Ginny and the bottle-breaker had finished off the night's accumulation and she came upstairs, Nick said he would give her and Anne a ride home; he brought his sports car around; Ginny held Anne, half asleep, on her lap and talked away with Nick. What was it like—working every night in a nightclub? Getting up on stage before a crowd?

"Tiring," he told her, adopting his weary, twenty-five going on seventy-five tone. "I should go to college—study philosophy—what do you think? Plato, Aristotle—they've gotta be easier than trying to earn a living off a nightclub."

"I'm sure you make plenty of money," she said.

He couldn't hold back a quick, proud smile. "Oh yeah, I guess I do all right."

Ginny reached around Anne to tweak his ear. "You're probably making a *ton* of money. Look at this car. You've got a brand-new sports car. And I always see pictures of your club in the papers. They write about the rich people who go there."

Nick smiled and thought to himself one of his favorite thoughts—yes, he *was* quite successful, and making a fair living, too. Twenty-five years old, never been to college, a new sports car. Club in the papers—his own name in the papers. Making as much as any doctor or lawyer his age, any Harvard grad.

After they'd taken Anne up to her apartment and were seated in the car again, Nick asked, "Now where?" meaning simply, Where did Ginny live?

"Do we have to go straight to my house?" she asked.

Nick looked over at her. It was almost three A.M. He had assumed he was just running these two girls home and then he was going to come right back to the club, go to sleep down in the basement room. Mary [one of his waitresses, with whom he sometimes spent the night] had said she would wait up for him.

"What did you have in mind?" he asked Ginny.

"Make a U-turn," she said.

He started the car, started to make the turn. "Why am I making a U-turn?" he asked.

"Take a right at the light," she said, leaning and pointing to the traffic signal up ahead. "Do you know Maloney's?"

"It's like a bowling alley?"

She nodded vigorously. "Twenty-four hours. We can get hamburgers there too."

Nick smiled, shook his head and took a right at the light. He glanced over at Ginny, her knees sticking out past the hem of her dress. He knew—even that first night going bowling he'd known—that she was not the type of girl he could go out and have fun with one night and then ignore. There was something unprotected, something lonely about her.

He had no need to go bowling, no need for hamburgers and no need really to go back to Mary who was just dutifully servicing him in the hope that eventually he would decide he loved her.

And then the fact was it was the longest and most relaxing vacation he'd had in years. Bowling, having a hamburger and a milk shake. Listening to Ginny talk away about her friends, her family, going fishing with her father; answering her questions about his business, his family. When she asked him if, in repayment for her bottle-breaking, he was going to let her come to the club for free the next night, he said, "Sure." And, at closing the next night, when she asked him where *he* was going to take *her* this time, he said she'd just have to wait and see.

More than thirty years later Mr. Pescadoor told his daughter Anne, to whom he has come to talk more openly and emotionally than to anyone else: "People have said to me—for instance, Ilena [one of his sisters, who, a few years after his marriage he brought out to the city to be his bookkeeper and general assistant]—Ilena has often made little, jealous remarks about how your mother was a strange woman to marry. Or said she doesn't have any more sense than a child. She's not a good mother, even. Imagine another woman saying that to a husband!

"We always had fun though. We seem to like one another, to get along. Sometimes I wonder what people are expecting from marriage. . . .

"In the beginning we used to work together. The way Ilena and I do now. I know as a housewife your mother is not the neatest, but she was very good at keeping after the clean-up at the club and at the first restaurant. Stocking—for a couple years she basically maintained the inventory.

"And, you know, she used to make me these incredible charts. Or schedules, I suppose you'd call them. In all these different colors. With symbols, keys, legends. They were supposed to help me organize my time, but mainly they'd have these big green and yellow blocks for when she and I were supposed to take time off together and go for a drive, or go out to eat—or I'd be scheduled to go to a particular department of a particular store where I'd have to buy her something costing at least so much money.

"I didn't mind. It was fun. Hell, I had plenty of cash then—I wasn't even paying rent anywhere, just living in the basement. And it was more the idea that I was supposed to do something for her—buy her something, be with her, take time off. That's what she liked—making the demand. And that's what I liked too—doing things for her, things she wanted me to do. Just being with her."

As he has always remembered it and tries, for amusement, to insist when his wife brings the debate up—it was she who proposed marriage. Eight months to the day after they met. Their "eight-month anniversary," she called it, and in honor of the occasion she had recommended he take her to Maloney's bowling alley where they'd gone on their first date. He had been perfectly willing to do so. And, as he remembers it, after they'd had their hamburgers she had told him to go to the counter and buy a package of cigars. Then she'd handed him one of the cigars and picked the other one up herself and, even though it was just a narrow, plastic-tipped cigar, she'd started rolling it between her fingers and sniffing it as if she was a connoisseur. "Nick," she had started to say in the huskiest voice she could come up with. Then she started giggling and couldn't say anything.

"What is going on?" he had asked.

She'd blurted it out—"You gotta marry me!"

At first he had assumed she meant she was pregnant, which was plausible since they were having sex regularly. He leaned toward her and asked, "Are you pregnant?"

She had blushed, put her head in her hands, shook her head vigorously.

He had had to pry her hands from around her face. "You're not pregnant?"

She had shaken her head again.

"You're not pregnant and I've *still* got to marry you."

She had grinned, nodded.

He had smiled, leaned back in his chair, bit the end off his cigar, lit it and got it started. He'd tilted his head to look at her out of the corner of his eye. "I'm not sure it's fair," he said. "If I haven't gotten you pregnant, I don't think I have to marry you. At least not the way I've always understood the rules."

She'd jumped up, come over to him and had shaken him by the shoulders. "Nick, stop teasing me! You're spozed to say yes. Get down on your knees, propose to me. Goddammit, Nick!"

He had gotten down on his knees, held his cigar in his right hand, taken her hand in his right hand. Looked up into her blushing face. "May I have this hand in marriage?" he had asked.

Ginny had nodded quickly, clapped her hands and run off and gotten some napkins so she could write out their guest list and wedding and honeymoon plans.

*

Knute's mother maintains—no matter in how much detail his father might be able to describe his fantasy of who said what at their fateful, eight-month anniversary trip to the bowling alley—nonetheless, he is wrong. She told him to buy the cigars, yes, but only because he wanted to teach her how to smoke one. Then he said something about needing an occasion for her first cigar. And he pulled out her diamond engagement ring, which she had no idea he'd bought. [Knute's father's version is that they bought the ring together later that morning.] Until Knute's father asked her to marry him, Knute's mother likes to say, she had no idea he was in love with her or she with him. The first night—she had just been curious about the club. The second night, when he invited her back—she did go back and without Anne—but that was just because Anne had to work at the hospital and because he told her it would be free—as payment for the bottle-breaking she'd done, was her

74

understanding. At the end of the night he offered to take her to an afterhours club. Why shouldn't she have gone? She'd never been to an afterhours club. Where there had been a huge, black saxophone player, and she had gotten too drunk, or too loud and clumsy anyway, on some very expensive French champagne that Knute's father kept ordering.

They were friends, they became friends. He had a sports car and often volunteered to take her driving in the country which she liked very much. He was very good about sitting in the car smoking cigars while she went skating. Sometimes he would even agree to get out of the car and walk out on the ice with her. Hold out his arms and she'd try to do pirouettes around him.

"The Happiest Years of My Life." When Knute was growing up his mother applied that label to the few years before and after her marriage, five, ten years before he was born. . . .

The old hospital gang piling into this one old car one of the other nurses had and driving to the beach. Then, after she started dating Knute's father, she still spent afternoons at the beach with her friends, but their father would take her there, alone, in his spiffy sports car.

And first he'd always fill the trunk with soda, tonic, bourbon, vodka—everything to mix drinks with. Plus, always, some treat that he'd refuse to tell her what it was until he presented it to the group. Chocolate, or expensive cigars for the men—something like that. . . .

There was a young doctor, Dr. Lester—he was a fabulous tennis player. He'd been nationally ranked in college. Mrs.

Pescadoor remembered back then that she was the only person at the hospital he'd play with. He had told her she was the only one who could keep up a steady rally with him and hit the ball hard enough.

Everybody used to go dancing, sledding, Christmas caroling in big groups. And there sure were some odd ducks in the bunch. Yours truly not included of course. . . .

Their first apartment. "I.e., heaven," Knute's sister once teased.

But no, Anne, please. She had found that apartment for their father and her right before they got married. It was five rooms on the second floor of a big house—they didn't have enough furniture for two rooms. And she had painted it all light yellow and light green. And it was very sunny. She bought the big yellow couch with the large green and blue flowers and matching footstools that, by the time Knute was old enough to notice it, had been relegated to the basement. When she was just married, though, it was practically their only furniture—or at least the only thing they had to sit on besides these two, ugly, metal and plastic chairs she'd found in the garage and given mouth-to-mouth, or scrub brush to dirt and rust. Luckily with some success—that was all they had to sit on when they ate in the kitchen. . . .

But it was a nice time, even just with that big couch. Their father worked very late, slept until just after noon. She'd stay up to see him when he came home, or sort of be half up, half asleep, with the radio on. But then—she had so much energy in those days, they wouldn't have recognized her. Kids. Kids had just beaten her down, that had to be it. Four or five in the morning she used to go to bed and be up before nine o'clock. Go out and do the shopping or work on one of her little projects: the painting she did all by herself, the flower beds she put in in front of the house on either side of the walk. She cleaned out the garage so there'd be a place for their father's car. Did Anne remember any of it? Probably not—she was only two when they'd moved. Nick Jr. would recognize it. He said he remembered the two baseball players she and Anne [her friend Anne] had tried to paint on his wall using this stencil thing. . . .

Those were the days. Their father didn't like having a real breakfast even then. Just his pot of coffee and his sweet roll. But she made sure he always had that. And she bought him the first of his elegant bathrobes. Red and black paisley. Satin. 'Cause he was a hot young nightclub owner then.

He'd sit on his personal end of the couch, his feet on one of the cushions. She'd get his coffee all set up for him on the little metal and glass antique table, the one that in Knute's day was usually by the newer couch, in the living room. She'd found it in an antique store one day when she was taking Nick Jr. for his morning constitutional in the stroller. Just two blocks away. In what was more a pawn shop than an antique store. . . .

It had been so nice in that room where the couch was. So sunny and open feeling. No buildings or trees. There were buildings but they were low and set back. The street was wide and just had little sprouts—little, scrawny trees that had just been planted. In a way that was something she didn't like about the two houses they'd had since then. It wasn't that there wasn't enough room. It's just that near the windows she always felt the big trees outside the walls. Or, in the first house Knute and Anne had lived in, there wasn't that much space on the sides, between their house and the neighbors. She hated that. It made her feel claustrophobic. Like she was in an airplane all the time.

But in that first apartment (as she remembered it) it was light, light, light. Light yellow. Knute's father would have his coffee on his china saucer from the set her since-deceased grandmother had given them. She'd be all over. (Knute's mother would be.) Sometimes lying down with her feet on his father's lap, getting in the way of him trying to be peaceful and wake up slowly. Or she'd have one of her butter and cheese sandwiches. Same as she always had. And Knute and Anne always teased her about.

They'd talk and talk. She'd talk. But she thought Knute's father liked that, he liked to just be there with her having made him his coffee and fussing over him and—talking away. About everything. It didn't really matter what. Her plans. For her little projects. What color should she choose for this room? Maybe a completely new color! She'd have to jump up and get the sample book to show him so they could pick. How much money did they have? One day she saw a beautiful breakfront, some rich, dark wood—mahogany maybe. She so much wanted to buy that. But that was one of the few times that

Knute's father said no, they couldn't afford it. It was very expensive, because it was an antique. Three hundred and forty dollars—that was a tremendous amount in those days.

Normally Knute's father was very generous with money. Knute knew that. He was too generous. He spent all his money on his family—and also sending checks to his father and to help his younger brother and sister get extra schooling. He earned a lot of money—for how old he was and when that was anyway—but . . . No, that's not really true. He spent some of the money he earned, but it was rarely wasted. Not counting going to their father's restaurants, they rarely ate out. They never took any trips, he always had to work. He had his dear friend Dan Cartwright, you know. [Dan Cartwright was Mr. Pescadoor's accountant.] Dan gave your father a lot of good investment advice. We've never saved a great deal, we don't have some huge pile of wealth. But we have a cushion. We have a beautiful house and the mortgage isn't that big. . . .

Marriage. (A subject easily rivaling the old apartment.) Before she met their father, Knute's mother liked to say, she had never really thought about marriage. She had been getting a little long in the tooth, but—she didn't notice anything when she was brushing. All those doctors, they were always trying to marry somebody, or something, plus perhaps another something on the side. She tried to stay out of it. She had Anne to tell her stories about true hospital romance.

But. When she—Mrs. Pescadoor—finally did get married! It was like going on a trip around the world. It seemed like such a perfect adventure. Knute's father paid all the bills. First she cut back to two nights a week at the hospital, then, after she got pregnant with Nick Jr., she quit altogether. She could buy things, decorate. As a girl growing up she hadn't been all that in love with buying things or decorating, but it was part of the adventure and that's what she liked.

When she had Knute's father on the couch there she used to tell him her visions of their future. He liked that, she felt. He'd ask her questions occasionally, maybe just to keep her talking, or at least to keep her on that subject. So what are we going to name all these kids we're going to make? This house—it comes with a swimming pool or I have to have one installed? And who rakes out the leaves? he'd joke.

And look—they had ended up—fifteen years later—with a swimming pool (which they had installed). A semi-circular gravel drive . . . What more could you want? She'd laugh.

As for all the kids. That was the strange part, a part that concerned, perplexed Mrs. Pescadoor when she talked about it. It had all been her doing, her decision. But. She didn't know. She'd had Nick Jr., had Anne. There'd been nothing wrong with them. Very healthy kids. Independent. Nick Jr. always had his friends to play football or war with. It was just a matter of getting him not to leave his plastic machine guns and grenades in the middle of the front hall floor. Anne had started playing the used upright piano that she, Mrs. Pescadoor, had rented for herself. Only three years old, she'd climb up on the bench, bang away—No, she played prettily even then. She was a marvel. She drew and made paintings, got perfect marks in school, went to her dance classes. And she played the piano so beautifully. It was like having a free concert every afternoon in your own living room.

She didn't know what it was. Often she thought it was the move out to the suburbs. Knute's father had been extremely busy then. He was always extremely busy, but during that period he was busier than usual because he'd recently sold out of the nightclub and started the first "Nick's Place." [As Mr. Pescadoor named the Italian restaurants he opened. By the time Knute was finishing elementary school his father had three Nick's Places. One in the city and one each in two smaller cities a few hours' drive away.]

At first—going on his own, no partner—having borrowed a lot of money—not having an established clientele—that was a lot for him to do. There was a big risk there, we could have lost it all. But—your father has a golden thumb when it comes to business. He's a natural.

But meanwhile. She had had to find them a house so there'd be room for Anne when she wanted to get out of her crib. And after she found the house she had to pack all their junk, supervise the moving. Then she'd had some of the stuff unpacked, other stuff still in boxes or covered with sheets in the middle of the room. So she could do the painting—after they had moved in. She didn't know why she'd thought she could do it that way—she had wanted to save money, to not be paying for an apartment and a mortgage at the same time.

She did do it. It took her almost a year. But she did it. Painted the whole inside of the house. Designed and shopped for cabinets and carpenters—everything. To bring that kitchen into the early twentieth century, if not the middle. She sewed and hung the curtains all by herself, even though sewing was the thing she hated more than almost anything in the world when she was a kid. . . . Sewed and hung the curtains . . . wallpaper, shades, plumbing problems, electrical problems, basement flooding problems—plus she'd had two very young kids to take care of. Anne had been with her all day while she was trying to do all this.

It was too much. Thinking back on it all, that was the one thing she was sure of—it had been too much. In one year she may have done more than most women. . . . Or more than was thought humanly possible. But she had paid through the nose for it.

Four, five years, she was basically exhausted. She didn't know what was wrong with her. She went to doctors, had the furnace checked three times! The doctors gave her pills. She tried each one once, then just left the bottles in her medicine chest. She still had them all. They filled up this one first-floor medicine chest in the new house—in a bathroom that was mainly just for guests, or for going to the bathroom when you were downstairs.

It was a strange time for her, she used to say. She was so tired during the days. Nick Jr. and Anne learned to make breakfast for themselves young. At dinner time she really was an awful mother. She couldn't think of anything to make. Even if she had food in the refrigerator. The kids were very good about it, especially Nick Jr., who would just get this stiff look on his face; he'd set his jaw, but never say anything more than "When's dinner going to be, Mom?" She'd tell him she wasn't sure, and he'd go back outside to play with his friends.

Anne would cry though. The later it got the more mournful her cries sounded. A lot of times Mrs. Pescadoor would finally just push her kids into the car, take them to a burger or pizza joint, or sometimes into the city to eat at Nick's. They could sleep in the office, she'd help the hostess seating the customers, or do the drink orders. When their father was ready to go home, they'd make a little two-car convoy, flashing their lights, racing one another sometimes.

She didn't know why, but late at night, when Knute's [future] father was due home, she had plenty of energy. That's when she did all the dishwashing, cleaning, toy-putting-away-ing, bed-making. In that one hour or so between eleven, eleven-thirty and when he came home—she was a superma-chine. She'd do what during the day would have taken her six, eight hours to do.

Then they'd take the dog out. Sam, the golden retriever Knute only really knew when he was getting into old age, after he'd lost a couple steps as they say in baseball.

She and Sam used to go for runs. Knute's father would walk along the sidewalk. She'd have Sam on the leash and they'd start running, go into the street where there were rarely any cars at that time of night. The dog could run a lot faster than she could. Her arm would be coming out of her socket, her legs would be going so fast it was like she was strapped to a possessed Exer-Bike.

It was great. Great exercise. All her muscles got stretched out. Her chest got filled with new, fresh air.

But. It didn't change how she felt in the mornings. She tried going swimming after she dropped the kids off at their schools. But she never liked swimming in pools, she had grown up swimming in a lake—she couldn't change. There's too much chlorine in pools. . . .

She tried a maid for a while. Thinking maybe—even though she didn't do anything all day except read dumb magazines. Still, maybe she was overworked somehow. She *was* overworked, from years earlier. Maybe she still had some resting to do from her wild, nursing days. Working a twelve-hour shift, going out dancing, sleeping two hours, working another twelve-hour shift.

She really didn't know what the problem was. She did know that a maid wasn't the answer. Or not that damn woman. She'd stolen at least one of her watches, one of Nick Jr.'s bicycles. He'd just gotten it for his birthday two weeks earlier. She told Knute's father he had to get rid of her, fire her—soon was not soon enough for that woman. . . .

And then she got pregnant with Knute. This is roughly the story she maintained. Happy years, then years in the doldrums and then, one day, one morning, pregnant with Knute. By accident. Not that she was trying very hard *not* to get pregnant. She wasn't trying very hard to do anything at that point. She'd been using contraception, but she'd sort of given it up. She and Mr. Pescadoor never had that much sex anyway. Sex wasn't on their top ten.

She just must have forgotten where she was in her cycle or something. Or the egg that had Knute's name on it wanted to come out early. Or overslept, came late.

She liked to tell Knute about the morning she discovered she was pregnant. An unseasonably warm February day, right around Valentine's Day. She went into the city to see her doctor. She had her suspicions, because—because she'd been late, very late. But she just remembered how warm even the buildings looked. How warm the doctor's hands felt. The smile he had on his face, like in a religious painting. Looking down on her.

She sprang right up and kissed him all over when he told her. No thought of her dignity—wearing only her birthday underwear.

She had driven straight from the doctor's to Nick's Place. First she'd let herself into the cellar and had gotten a magnum—a very large bottle—of champagne. Just Knute's father and Ilena were there. Knute's father was having his coffee and sweet roll, waking up.

Guess what! she had said to them. They had to guess why she had brought the big bottle of champagne over from the cellar. What was the good news?

Ilena guessed pretty quickly because Knute's father had mentioned to her that she [Knute's mother] was coming into the city that morning to go see her doctor. Ilena wouldn't keep her mouth shut and let Knute's father try to guess. She was a spinster and, therefore, Knute's mother maintained, Ilena was always criticizing her to Knute's father.

*

After hints from his wife and Ilena's quips though, Mr. Pescadoor did guess. "You're pregnant!"

Mrs. Pescadoor nodded and ran to him and jumped into his lap. Got up and started dancing around the room singing, "I'm gonna have a baby, I'm gonna have a baby."

At first Mr. Pescadoor wasn't sure what to think. He knew that when they'd first gotten married his wife had talked a lot about having a big family, perhaps eight kids such as there were in her family. Then, shortly after they'd moved to the suburbs, from the apartment to the house, she'd announced that she didn't want to have any more kids. He'd been a little disappointed about that. Her talks about big families had led him to imagining big Christmas dinners, coming home to see his sons playing touch football on the front lawn, sons-in-law, daughters-in-law, grandchildren. But his wife had said she thought two kids were more than enough for her, she couldn't be the kind of full-time supermother her mother had been. What could he say? It wouldn't have been right for him to say, No, I insist you get pregnant again, I want more children, make more kids. Among other things, he did spend many,

many hours every week with his restaurant business. She was the one who raised the children.

And now she was pregnant again. That certainly seemed to please her, judging by all the dancing and singing she was doing. If it pleased Ginny, Knute's father thought, that was the best thing.

Chapter 3

On a Thursday afternoon in the middle of the March of Knute's sixth-grade year he was up in his room, lying on his stomach on his bed, reading his social studies book. It was his favorite book that winter. As a way of describing how people lived in the different regions of the U.S., for each region it presented a fictional white family. For New England there was a Mr. Potter, a Maine lobsterman, his wife, son and daughter. For the mid-Atlantic states Mr. Barney, a New York stock trader, plus wife, son and daughter. The Great Lakes had Mr. Smith, a Detroit assembly-line worker and union steward, along with wife, two kids. There were pictures showing the husbands at work; the wives talking with neighbors, postmen, pharmacists; the kids at school or helping with the household chores. There were conversations about the weather, how rapidly the world was changing, whether or not to strike.

For Knute it was a bit like reading a story—entering into

other people's worlds, taking on their worries and hopes. But the book's classification—social studies textbook—made him sure it wasn't just some writer's fantasy. Mr. and Mrs. Potter and Johnny and Sue existed. He knew that when he went to Maine, he'd see them. And he didn't feel any need to visit Maine right away. He was quite satisfied lying on his bed afternoons and evenings, having Mr. Potter on the pages open beneath him, again—as in previous days and weeks—hefting his catch from his boat to the dock, telling the lobster fisherman standing there how important it was that they not take out more lobsters than were hatching each year.

"Knute, how would you like to do me a big favor?" his mother called from the bottom of the stairs. "I forgot to get Parmesan cheese at the supermarket this morning. I need some if I'm going to make the lasagna the way you like it. Do you think—"

"OK," Knute didn't let her finish the question. No point wasting words. They both already knew that, as on most of the previous afternoons, he was going to go get what his mother had forgotten to get. He got off his bed and came down the stairs, hardening his features as he generally did to show his mother he found no pleasure in her forgetfulness or in coming to her rescue. He stuck out his hand for her to put the money for the cheese in. He got his bike from the garage, rode to the store and got the cheese.

Toward the end of dinner that night his mother asked him what his plans were for the evening.

"Go read," Knute said.

"You don't want to work on the puzzle?" A few weeks earlier Knute had been home with the flu and his mother had bought a picture puzzle for them to work on. The pieces were spread out on the other end of the dining table, not a whole lot of them joined to other pieces.

Knute glanced at the picture. It was a Dutch scene; two windmill arms were taking shape near the top edge. He shook his head. "I'd rather read."

"If you'd always rather read, how are we ever going to get that puzzle done?"

"Maybe you'll have to finish it without me." He got up from the table, took his dishes into the kitchen.

"You're not even having any of the ice cream I bought?"

Knute pushed through the swinging door into the kitchen. He was developing the method, when he didn't want to play with his mother, of saying very little and trying to slip away.

His mother came into the kitchen. "At least you'll help me with the dishes, I hope. After all the hours I put in making you that lasagna!"

He didn't say anything, but he brought all the dishes to the counter by the sink and the dishwasher, and then worked away till the smaller dishes were rinsed and in the machine, the pots washed by hand and stacked in the drying rack. "I'm gonna go read now," he said. "Thanks for the good lasagna."

"Knute," his mother said as he was walking out of the kitchen.

"What?"

"Oh, I don't know. I don't know, Knute. There isn't anything wrong is there, you're not mad at me?"

Mrs. Pescadoor's confidence was more shaky than usual that year. The previous summer Anne had gotten her driver's license and Mr. Pescadoor had bought her a brand-new white car. It seemed to Mrs. Pescadoor that Anne was always out, or running out the door. Staying late at the studio at school making paintings. Late dinners at the pizza parlor with her friends. Going to Chicago with her art teacher. Mrs. Pescadoor told herself she was happy that Anne had plans for her life—ambition. And she accused herself of never having had any.

And there was Knute's flu. That October when she had taken him to the pediatrician for his semi-annual check-up, the doctor had recommended giving him a flu shot because he had heard a particularly virulent flu strain was expected to cross the Midwest that winter. But Mrs. Pescadoor had said no. And, not just no—she had said it was ridiculous—kids were being given too many shots, a little flu never hurt anyone.

And so, finally, in early March, Knute had gotten a particularly bad case of this particularly virulent flu. He was home for nine days, for two of those days his fever had stayed up dangerously high. Mrs. Pescadoor had been worried for his life; she'd had the pediatrician come visit twice.

An ex-nurse even, making her own kid get so sick like that! she cursed herself. She kept recalling certain lines she'd spoken to the pediatrician in rejecting the shot: "If it ain't broke, don't fix it, right?" "The kid can spend a couple days in bed—

watch all the game shows if need be." "Did you forget I'm an ex-nurse, Dr. Danforth? If I ever had any illusions about current medical practice, I lost them long ago."

Why couldn't she have just said, "Yes, Dr. Danforth, if you think the shot is called for, you're the doctor, give him the shot."

But no. Always her little, stupid opinions. Butting in, ruining things, hurting people. So many mistakes, embarrassments, bad memories. She remembered how, some years earlier, Anne's lower back had gotten infected after someone fell on her at school. And she [Mrs. Pescadoor] had said for a whole weekend it was just a bruise. There was the time she'd tried to get Nick Jr. not to go back to playing football after his knees started swelling up. There she'd been definitely trying to look out for his health. But it seemed like she'd just ended up embarrassing him in front of his coach and making him angry at her.

She was a terrible mother. She had come to this conclusion before and would come to it again. (And, previously she had decided, and in the future she would decide, she was an excellent mother—or at least better than any of the other mothers she knew.) That winter, though, she was sure: She was a terrible mother.

This Thursday night Knute told her he wasn't mad at her, he just wanted to read.

"You just wanna read every night these days," she said.

He shrugged. He wasn't conscious of the change, but he had been spending more time in his room reading since his illness.

He preferred staying out of the way of his mother's moping; her questions: "Be honest with me, Knute, on a scale of one to ten, how would I rate compared with other mothers you know?" "Am I really the best mother you've ever had?"

As he went up the stairs she called to him and when he looked back she was making a mournful face, and she said in a mournful tone, "Look at him—leaving his mother all alone. With so few of her puzzle pieces put together. Even a couple of the edge pieces still not found."

"Mom." He turned away and continued mounting the stairs, now with greater speed.

"Mom what?" his mother asked from below.

"You know."

"I know what?"

"Come on, I just wanna read."

"Come on yourself." Mrs. Pescadoor turned and walked slowly to the kitchen, made herself a sundae.

The next afternoon she showed up in the parking circle after school and when Knute got in the car announced, "Knute, I feel bad for making you do all those dishes last night and keeping you from that book you seem to love so much. I want to do something to make it up to you."

Knute could see she was headed toward the road that led to the interstate. They were going into the city. He leaned on his elbow on the arm of his door, looked out the window.

"Remember how I promised at Christmas I would get you new hockey skates?"

He didn't say anything.

93

"Knute?"

He nodded.

"I called Greschner's today. They say they've got your size. They're holding them for us. How's that!"

"Hmm," Knute said. He saw the rest of the day—driving into the city, going to three or four stores at the shopping center, then to the Chinese restaurant his mother liked to go to, then over to his father's restaurant for a couple hours. Home, maybe, by eleven. He thought to himself that what he hated was how it was always the same, he always knew what his mother was going to do. What he also felt, but at twelve years old was far from finding words for, was the sense of pointlessness and disconnection that dogged his mother. He didn't as much mind going round and round in circles with her as he was afraid of what her behavior suggested—that there wasn't anything else to do.

She reached and tweaked his ear. "You're not excited to be getting new skates?"

Did she really want to know his opinion? No. At the moment he wasn't at all excited to be getting new skates. He stared out the window.

"Mom to Knute, Mom to Knute, come in Knute."

"What?"

"Aren't you excited to be getting new skates!"

"Why?" he asked.

"Why? What kind of a question is that? New hockey skates! Don't you keep saying how your skates are too small, they give you blisters?"

"They are too small." He watched the lawns, driveways,

houses, repair shops go by. The television station with its towers just before they got to the highway.

"Think of the poor kids in China who don't even have hockey skates. . . . Think of the new skates Doug just got—that's the kind I'm getting you. The creme de la creme. You'll be the fastest skater on the team now, I'll bet!"

He wouldn't be the fastest skater on the team; silently to himself Knute corrected his mother's statement. Doug was and always would be the fastest skater on the team, and by quite a bit. Because of his height, what he [Knute] could do was score goals. Stand on one side of the net and, having longer arms than most of the other kids, he found it easy enough to sweep the puck past the goalie. After Doug passed it to him.

"Cat got your tongue?" his mother asked. "What did you do in school today? Tell me everything you learned."

"Maybe later."

"Later, later, later. What am I supposed to do now—drive like a maniac?" She started turning the wheel back and forth rapidly so the car swerved a bit and rocked.

"Mom."

"There you go with that mom stuff. What do you think—it's your job to keep me from having fun? Last night no puzzle, now no highway wreck. Boy you're a bore, Knute."

Knute couldn't quite keep from smiling at that last speech. What could he do? he felt. It didn't matter what he did. His mother had the car, the car keys. And nothing would stop her from chattering away, making joke after joke. He could either cover his ears with his hands or laugh.

For the rest of the afternoon and the first part of the evening he went with the latter option. They bought skates—not the same kind as Doug had—indeed, as Knute had thought, those had to be ordered specially from a Canadian manufacturer. But his mother insisted that the skates they bought were even nicer than Doug's, at least they looked nicer.

They bought themselves ten pairs of socks too, five for each. Two hockey sticks. Three pucks. Matching black and orange jackets. They went to the Chinese restaurant, and then they made a brief stop at Nick's Place. Around nine they headed home.

As they brought their purchases into the front hall Mrs. Pescadoor suggested having some of the ice cream she'd bought for the night before, then going to work on the puzzle. "Do we have to?" Knute asked.

"No, we don't *have to*, but I thought it would be fun."

"How about tomorrow night? I just feel like reading tonight. I'm too tired to work on that puzzle."

Mrs. Pescadoor suggested he read in the kitchen. She'd make hermits, his favorite. They'd bring the big chair from the living room into the kitchen. While she made the hermits he could read, maybe he'd even want to read aloud to her the way she always enjoyed so much. It seemed like he really liked his social studies book, probably she'd like it too.

"That chair's too heavy," Knute said. "It's too bulky."

"No it's not. Come. Come in the living room with me. You'll see. I'll carry it all by myself. You can just take the footstool."

"Mom, remember you tried to do this once before," Knute said in a whiny tone, following his mother into the living room. "We ended up having to go around outside. Don't you remember?"

"No. Watch." She hitched her pants up and then crouched down like a weightlifter, behind the chair. More for comedy than to try and pick up the big armchair, she wrapped her long arms around the back and clasped them in front, her hands gripping her forearms. She grunted loudly. And with some jerking of her legs, back and arms, she lifted the chair a few inches off the ground twice. Then let go. So it dropped and bounced on the rug. "Whew, see how easy that was?" She laughed. Put her hands on her lower back. "Zee gods. I guess I'm not as strong as I used to be. I hope I didn't throw any disks anywhere."

"Mom. I'm going to go read."

"Knute! Come on. Don't be such a spoilsport. Maybe I can't lift the chair myself, but if you say we got it in the kitchen before, why can't we do it again?"

"I don't want it in the kitchen."

"You *do* want it in the kitchen. You just don't realize it. Seriously Knute, it's Friday night. You can't just go up to your room and leave your mother down in the kitchen making hermits all by hermits. I mean, by herself. I mean listen to the word, Knute—hermits. It even sounds lonely."

"Fifteen minutes. I'll help you with this silly chair and then I'll read there for fifteen minutes. Then I'm going up to my room."

"Half an hour."

"No. Fifteen minutes."

"But I can hardly even get the eggs out of the fridge in fifteen minutes."

"Mom, I'm tired."

"Oh come on, Knute. It's hardly nine o'clock. Another half-hour won't kill you. Tomorrow's Saturday, you can sleep late."

"I can't sleep late," Knute corrected his mother. "Saturday is hockey practice, remember? At eight-thirty."

"Oh so what! You go to bed at eleven, you can get eight hours sleep and be up at seven."

"Mom," he said under his breath. He started toward the hall. "Half an hour is absolutely the limit." He went to the front door, yanked it open. Went through the kitchen to the back door, yanked it open. Walked back to the living room. Picked up the stool and carried it into the kitchen. Went back to the living room. "OK, Mom. You take the back, I'll take the legs."

"Yessir."

They got the chair into the kitchen. Set it up by the door to the basement, where it would be out of the way of Mrs. Pescadoor's cooking. Knute got his social studies book. Started to read about the Great Lakes region and Mr. Smith, the Detroit autoworker. But he didn't enjoy the reading at all. It was, or until that moment it had been, his book, something—a group of people—he was involved with apart from his mother. Now the spell had been broken. He felt sad, regretful. His voice dragged as he read. In the middle of the second paragraph he stopped. "I can't read out loud anymore, Mom," he said.

"Oh why? I was just getting interested. How many cars go

by on the line every hour and how long it is, that's very interesting. It makes you realize how organized everything has to be to make a car."

Knute nodded, but didn't say anything. He was reading to himself.

"You're really not going to keep reading aloud?"

He shook his head, kept reading to himself.

"Oh, I'm so disappointed. I thought you said you were going to read to me for a half-hour."

Knute didn't hear this. He was lost in his reading.

Mrs. Pescadoor went about getting her dishes and ingredients out, starting to prepare the batter. And she made slightly more noise than usual. More than once metal bowls knocked into one another. The electric mixer had to be tested a few times. . . .

Plus there was the intermittent commentary. "Here I am, married, mother of three, all alone on a Friday night. . . . All alone, except for my youngest son, who'd rather read about a man bolting things on an assembly line than play with his mother. . . . Ah, well, la-dee-da. . . . The boy's poor mother is working so hard, all by herself, to make him hermits, his favorite dessert. . . . And he could help her—if he were a nicer boy. . . . But no. Rather read his book. His social studies textbook. On a Friday night. . . . Ah well. . . . He's gonna end up a complete bore, working in some dark, dusty library, with no friends. . . . Even though his mother tried her best to stop him. . . . Make him hermits. . . . La-dee-da . . ."

Knute heard enough of these comments and the banging to know his mother was trying to regain his attention. And he sensed she wasn't going to be quiet unless he started reading aloud again, or worked on the puzzle with her, or whatever.

His mother turned on the radio.

"Mom." He looked up from the book at her. Wasn't there some way he could just read his book?

"I'm turning it down, I'm turning it down. Don't worry."

He got up. "I'm going to read in my room." He started out of the room.

"Just because I turned on the radio? I'm sorry if it was loud when it came on, I said I was going to turn it down."

Knute didn't say anything, headed up the stairs.

His mother came to the bottom of the stairs, called up after him. "What's going on? Did I do something to upset you? I hope I . . . I didn't mean to upset you." She started up the stairs quickly.

"I'm gonna go read in my room, Mom."

"What happened to my half-hour?"

"It disappeared."

"It's not even ten o'clock. You said you were going to read to me."

Knute had lain down on his stomach on his bed, opened his book again. "Mom," he said. "I decided I didn't want to."

"Why not? You said you'd read to me for a half-hour. Then you stopped after less than a minute. Why? You're not angry with me are you? I didn't do anything wrong?"

"Mom. Please. Just go make the hermits."

"Just go make the hermits! Listen how he talks to his mother." She switched to one of her comic voices, a pinched, nyeah-nyeah tone. "You just go make my hermits. I wanna read by myself in my room. When the hermits are done you can call me. I'll come down to eat them. Then I'll just wanna read my book in my room again."

"Mom." He got up off the bed, took his book and walked past his mother, out of his room and down the hall to his brother's room. His brother being away at college, the room was hardly used, except as a place for storing his childhood memorabilia and things he no longer needed.

Knute locked the door behind him, went and sat in the armchair, and opened his book.

His mother coming after him heard the lock. Still she tried to open the door and said, "You've locked me out?"

"Just go downstairs, Mom."

"Just go downstairs, Mom! Now he's ordering me around!" She beat on the door with her fists. Then said quietly, "He's locked me out."

Knute stayed in his seat, his back to the door. For a few moments his mother remained standing right by the door. He tried to start reading again. He heard his mother at his back. He heard—or imagined hearing—her exhaling against the door. He sensed her mind churning, trying to figure out her next move.

At first, standing by the door, Mrs. Pescadoor was overcome by the feeling of having been locked out. She had a sense of the size of her house, its twelve rooms, ten-foot ceilings. And no one anywhere. Except for her youngest child who had locked himself in this one corner room.

She wandered into the bathroom, sat on the toilet seat. Her

left elbow on the edge of the sink. Left hand supporting her head. It seemed there was nothing to do but wait there for someone, maybe her husband, to come home and rescue her. A tear started from her left eye, slid across her cheek and then ran along the seam between her little finger and her face.

And then it came to her. The perfect idea! The perfect way to get Knute to unlock the door—and to have some fun!

She pulled out the plastic bucket that was under the sink and removed the cleaning supplies kept inside it. She filled the bucket with water from the bathtub spigot, returned to Nick Jr.'s door and called cheerfully to Knute inside, "I guess I've gotta flood you out." Then she threw the water against the bottom of the door.

"Mom!" Knute shouted, jumped up from his chair and started for the door. He saw some of the water soaking into the carpet, coloring it a darker blue.

"You didn't expect me to do that did you!"

He shook his head but didn't say anything. He retreated from the door and went over to his brother's bed by the windows looking out across the driveway, the half-moon of dirty-snow-covered lawn; sidewalk; tree trunks; the street. He lay down on the bed on his stomach. Head turned from the door, toward the windowsills. It was just a matter of waiting for his mother to do something more extreme.

"I still haven't flushed you out?" she shouted from the bathroom where she was refilling the bucket. "Try this!" she shouted when she threw the second bucketful against the door.

"Mom, cut it out," Knute said as much to the windowsills as to his mother.

"I won't cut it out until you come out and read to me for a half-hour like you promised," she answered, and at the end Knute heard the sounds of the words fading as she turned and headed back to the bathroom. He heard the water running in the tub again. He scrambled off the bed, marched over, unlocked and opened the door, and stepped into the hall. "What is the matter with you! You wanna ruin our house?"

"It's only water," she called from the tub where she was still filling her bucket.

"Water can do a lot of damage." He went back in his brother's room, got his book, came back out. His mother came rushing out of the bathroom, left hand holding the rim of the bucket, right hand under the bottom; prepared to dump again. "Look," he said, gesturing to the bottom of the door which was wet. "You're probably gonna have to repaint that."

He walked past her and back into his room. Lay back down on his bed, opened his book. His mother was right behind him with her bucket. "I'm probably going to have to repaint you," she said, laughing and—just as he jerked his head up—dumping the water out in the direction of where his head had been.

Because he'd moved, Knute didn't get much water on his head, just on his arms, all over his bed, *and*—all over his book. He took one look at it, the pages swelling with water, then grabbed one edge and hurled it at his mother's legs. Tears came to his eyes. "You are such a jerk," he said. Got off the bed again. "You just wreck everything." His muscles quivered, he wanted both to lash out and regain control of himself.

"I am so sick of you!" he said. "You waste your own life, you waste your house, and then you just try to waste everyone else." He walked past her again. Down the hall, around the corner past his brother's room. Down to his parents' bedroom. He paused deciding which of his mother's possessions he wanted to get. Then he walked to his mother's bureau. Opened the top drawer and took out her Chinese black-and-red lacquered jewelry box.

His mother had followed him into her room, and now he turned and passed her again, going across the hall to the little sewing, sitting, shoe storage or shoebox storage room there. With strength he had never before manifested, with his left hand he picked up the wooden chair that was behind the sewing table and he kept thrusting the legs of the chair at one of the windows until he had made holes in its lower pane and in the lower pane of the storm window. Then he stepped back and hurled the box as hard as he could through the window and out toward the drive. He turned back toward his mother. "You destroy something that's precious to me, I destroy something that's precious to you."

"Oh you do, hunh!" she said, a big smile spreading on her face. "I think you just better hope you can finish what you've just started." She laughed, a cackling laugh that Knute had never heard before. She turned and went down the hall to Knute's bedroom. Leaning over the bed, she took hold of the clock-radio Knute kept on the shelf there. With a yank she pulled it off the shelf, the plug out of the wall. She turned back again. Stooped to pick up Knute's social studies book. Carried the two objects, one in each hand, down the hall past Knute again, into the sewing room. She set them on the sewing table, and, with Knute standing watching in the doorway, she picked up the chair with both hands and thrust repeatedly at the broken windows until she'd made very large holes. Then she shoveled the clock radio and the book out.

Knute listened to his clock-radio and his book moving through the air—somewhere far out in space it seemed—then smashing on the cement floor of the porch below. He smiled, turned and walked quickly into his parents' bedroom, into the master bath. He opened the doors of both medicine chests. Looked from one to the next, surveyed the objects—bottles of perfume and cologne, Q-tips, razors. . . . He turned to the nearest cabinet, the one over the toilet, and gathered in his arms, like a load of oranges, as many of the items as he could. His mother's or his father's—he wasn't selective. He walked past his mother again. Back into the sewing room. Dumped his load of products out the broken window. Listened with his mother to the cracking, crackling sounds as some of the glass bottles broke on the porch.

Mrs. Pescadoor laughed. Her raspy laugh. It wasn't a prolonged laugh. Just a note or two. Very dry on account of the cigarettes she smoked. Then she walked briskly to Knute's room. Pulled down the huge color poster of an ice-hockey star which she had bought for him. Balled it up a little, took it to the sewing room and tossed it out.

Knute took the two bedside lamps from his parents' bedroom and brought them to the window and pitched them out. His mother listened to the crashes, then headed down the hall, pulled out the top drawer of Knute's bureau, which, by tilting it on a diagonal, she managed to get out the window.

Knute next selected his mother's shoes. His mother chose

his schoolbooks and notebooks. Since the master bedroom was a good deal closer to the window than Knute's room was, he began making almost two trips to each of hers. She tried running to catch up, but then Knute started running, increasing his advantage to better than two to one.

*

Clothes, pillows, sheets, memorabilia—as in a clearance sale, everything had to go. And everything might have—the two rooms might have been emptied of all but the largest pieces of furniture—and then perhaps Knute and his mother would have gone on to work on clearing out the sewing room, or his brother and sister's rooms. Were it not for Mr. and Mrs. Neighbor and their children.

The Mr. and Mrs. Neighbor title was Knute's mother's. The Lefferts, as they were otherwise known, lived on one side of the Pescadoors. They were a family of six headed by Mrs., a part-time lawyer, and Mr., a mechanical engineer. When the Pescadoors first moved onto the street, this couple and their children had been by far the most welcoming. They had offered to lend lawn equipment, carpentry or painting tools, ladders; to pick anything up at the store that the busy new arrivals might need. Many evenings that first and the second summer one of the children had come over to see if any of the Pescadoors wanted to join their backyard cocktail party or buffet, or just have some coffee and dessert with them on their front porch.

Some weekday mornings Mrs. Lefferts would invite Mrs. Pescadoor over for coffee. She'd make toast too and put every-thing—butter, cream, sugar, a whole pot of coffee—on a tray which they'd take out to the table underneath the big tree in the Lefferts' backyard. Mrs. Lefferts would pour them each their coffees, wait for Mrs. Pescadoor to mix in her cream and sugar, and then sit back, eyeing Mrs. Pescadoor up and down as if she wanted to make sure she was properly dressed before they started talking.

"So tell me," was a typical Mrs. Lefferts opening. Which, for instance, on one occasion had been followed by: "Nick Jr. is going to which college?" "He wasn't interested in any of the Eastern schools?" "What is he studying?" "He's planning to go work with his father in the restaurant business?" Or, on another occasion: "You said you worked as a nurse, Ginny?" "In what hospital was it?" "Did you ever consider going back to work?" "How about getting your college degree?" On another day it was: "Where did you say your family was from again?" And so forth.

After Ginny gave her answers, Mrs. Lefferts would look her in the eye, nod and say something sympathetic: "Yes, it isn't easy to raise kids and run a household." "Yes, I think it's al-ways sad when the first one leaves."

Mrs. Pescadoor loved going over and having coffee and toast and talking with Mrs. Lefferts. It was like in the old days, going down to the coffee shop with Anne. It was like they were alone on the edge of the earth. And she could say everything she had been thinking. And it seemed that Mrs. Lefferts was truly interested in and concerned for her life and family. It seemed like she was asking all these questions because she wanted to help her in some way.

Yet, Mrs. Pescadoor didn't generally think of herself as someone who needed or was looking for help. She had the [accurate] sense that information was being collected from her; that on the basis of this information judgments, often critical and seemingly final, were being made; and that both information and judgments were being passed on, from Mrs. Neighbor to Mr., the children, friends and other neighbors. After the conversations Knute's mother always felt a little uneasy, exposed.

On the night of the big fight, the Lefferts were playing Scrabble in their front study. Hearing the faint sounds of some of the heavier and/or more breakable items—books, bottles, lamps—hitting the porch, the Lefferts began to wonder if something unusual might be going on next door. Then Knute threw his mother's little television out, and, when it hit the cement, the tubes exploded. Mrs. Neighbor got up from the Scrabble game and the whole family followed her out onto their front porch. They listened for a few moments. Heard the rather gentle sound of four of Knute's sweaters falling onto the yews that separated the porch from the drive. Then Mr. Pescadoor's electric razor and aftershave making a more definitive sound.

Mrs. Neighbor glanced at Mr. Neighbor and silently they agreed it would be remiss of them not to go investigate. Mrs.

herded the children back into the house, and all put on their coats and went back out and over to the Pescadoor's.

They rang the bell, but Knute and his mother didn't hear it. And a few more objects came out the window and joined the large and disorderly pile on the porch to the Lefferts' left. After the second, a sewing machine, hit, Mrs. Lefferts quickly stepped forward, turned the knob with a jerk, threw the door open. She walked across the front hall to the bottom of the stairs. "Ginny," she called. "What in God's name is going on!"

There was no reply, neither Mrs. Pescadoor nor Knute having heard Mrs. Lefferts.

Like a commando leader in a television drama, Mrs. Lefferts, without looking back at her family, motioned with her arm for them to follow her. Into the front hall/swamp. She briskly mounted the stairs. As she got to the top she saw Mrs. Pescadoor running down the hall to Knute's room to get another load. "Ginny," she barked.

Ginny jumped, frightened. Her right shoulder knocked against the wall.

Mrs. Lefferts stood still, watching, waiting while Mrs. Pescadoor regained her balance, blinked her eyes.

"It's just me, Joyce, Ginny," Mrs. Lefferts spoke very slowly, quietly, and started slowly coming up the last five stairs. She had the idea that she knew exactly how to deal with people who had become over-emotional. The key, I will say (though of course she wouldn't) (but her strategy may nonetheless have been ideal)—the key was to be completely patronizing. Treat the upset individual like a five-year-old grandchild, no matter what his or her actual age or kinship was.

"There's no need to be upset anymore," Mrs. Lefferts said. Slowly, quietly, steadily, moving forward. "I'm here. . . . We can just take it easy now."

Mrs. Pescadoor put her hand to her forehead and then pulled her hand back, pulling her scarf off, out of her hair. She used the scarf to wipe the sweat off her face.

There were sounds from around the corner and out on the porch as Knute chucked a china lamp.

"Knute, come here," Mrs. Lefferts said sternly, but did not shout.

"Knute," Mrs. Pescadoor said, as if she'd just remembered him. She leaned her head to the wall, looked over at Mrs. Lefferts who was still slowly approaching her, and said quietly, "Jeez, what has been going on around here?"

"It's OK, everything's going to be all right now," Mrs. Lefferts said, still advancing.

With both hands Mrs. Pescadoor pressed her scarf to her eyes, and she started crying.

Mrs. Lefferts took hold of her upper arms. "It's OK, everything's going to be all right now."

Knute came around the corner, wondering who had yelled for him. He saw his mother holding her scarf to her face and sobbing. The significantly shorter Mrs. Lefferts gripping his mother's arms. Keeping her from collapsing onto the floor. Whispering to her. "It's OK, Ginny. Everything's going to be all right now."

"Mrs. Lefferts," Knute said. As if it was a guess, or an answer. A man in a blazer and holding a microphone had come up to him in his second-floor hallway. "Look at the camera and tell our audience at home in five seconds or less the true name of this woman in the raincoat with the fur collar who's standing next to you, holding up your mother who's sobbing uncontrollably."

"Mrs. Lefferts," Knute had said. He had guessed right. Then he sat down against the other wall, across from his mother. He felt exhausted. His arms and legs heavy, his vision a little cloudy. His mother seemed to be crying in a neighboring house. Not right next to him in the hall.

Mrs. Lefferts called for her daughter Andrea and told her to take Knute downstairs, "maybe get him something to drink. Whatever he wants. And tell the others to start bringing the stuff in from outside. Especially those things that can be saved. You can spread some newspapers in the hall there. So the mud won't get all over everywhere."

Knute got up as seemed to be required. He let Andrea take his hand and walked down the stairs with her. He chose root beer for his drink.

For the next hour or so Knute and Andrea sat in the dining room, shared three cans of root beer, and talked about his sixth-grade teacher and school experiences and her ninth-grade teachers and experiences. In other rooms of the house, the other Lefferts went through their maneuvers. Mrs. Lefferts took Mrs. Pescadoor to her bedroom. Helped her off with her shoes, pants and sweater and had her lie under the covers. She called for her youngest to run home and get a few bags of chamomile and make Mrs. Pescadoor some tea. She sat on the bed next to Mrs. Pescadoor, rubbed her legs under the blanket and pulled away the strands of hair that fell onto her tear-soaked face. While keeping up a monologue about how it was OK, there was no need to get upset anymore, what was done was done. "We'll feel better tomorrow. . . ." "You just got angry and things got out of hand, that's all. . . ."

The other Lefferts children besides Andrea brought everything inside, wiped things off, put them on newspapers. They put the beginnings of the hermit batter away in the refrigerator and washed the dishes. At his mother's request, John, the only son, called Nick's Place in the city. Explained the events to Mr. Pescadoor and explained that his [John's] mother wanted him [Mr. Pescadoor] to come home right away.

Mr. Lefferts, following his own orders, came upstairs to inspect the broken window in the sewing room. In one of the drawers of the sewing table he found a tailor's tape which he used to determine the dimensions of the window. Then he went back to his basement workshop and made a plywood panel to cover the hole. He came back with his panel and a lot of his tools. Pulled out the remaining pieces of glass, inserted the panel and tacked it to the window frame. Picked the larger pieces of glass out of the carpet, found the vacuum cleaner and vacuumed the room.

Two policemen came. A neighbor across the street called them when he heard the television explode. The police came about a half-hour later. When Mrs. Lefferts heard them talking to her son and oldest daughter in the front hall, she excused herself from Mrs. Pescadoor's care momentarily and went downstairs. "Everything's under control. There've been no crimes here," she said. And she herded the two men out, back to their patrol car in the driveway. She tried to send them off on their rounds again. She didn't want to create any more of a scene, any more embarrassment for Ginny Pescadoor. Or at least that was her sense of why she had to concern herself with the police.

The two officers allowed themselves to be ushered out and back to their car, but then they didn't get in it and drive off. They didn't have anything else to do except drive around the neighborhood. So they reported in to headquarters on their radio, switched off their rotating red light and came back up on the porch. Tried out the rocking sofa there. Admired it and the luxury of the property—the French doors of the living room, the porch screened from the street by the tall yews. Plants in cement urns. Semi-circular gravel drive. Full-acre lot instead of the usual quarter-acre or less.

When the clean-up was finished, the eldest Lefferts daughter came out and asked the men if they wanted coffee. "Never hurts," they agreed. So, with Knute's help, the Lefferts children found Mrs. Pescadoor's coffee, percolator pot and dishes. Brought the men some fresh-brewed coffee, with three Fig Newtons decorating each of the saucers.

*

When Mr. Pescadoor came home this was the first thing he noticed—these two policemen sitting on his porch lounger,

holding saucers and drinking coffee. He went over and introduced himself, asked how things stood inside. The men assured him everything was under control, the neighbors had
done some cleaning up, put his wife and maybe his son too to
bed. Just a little Friday night excitement, they said.

Mr. Pescadoor said he was glad to hear that and he thanked
the men for coming by on a busy night just to make sure. "I
guess I'd better go inside, see how things stand, let the neighbors go home to bed."

The police nodded approvingly, sipped some more on their
coffees. "Mind if I ask you something?" the younger of the
two men said as Mr. Pescadoor was turning to go inside.

Mr. Pescadoor shook his head.

"One of the neighbor girls said you were Nick, of the Nick's
Places. The restaurants. I don't mean to embarrass you or anything, but is that right?"

Mr. Pescadoor smiled. Slipped into one of his routines.
"You watch my commercials?" he asked. (Referring to the
commercials that ran on television late at night. They featured
him standing in one of his restaurants, smiling, talking about
his food, holding up plates of it, and bringing his cooks and
some of his waitresses on camera and introducing them.)

In response to the question, the two policemen, looking over
from the lounger, nodded. The younger one said, "Sometimes.
When I'm not working."

"So," Mr. Pescadoor said. "Do I look like me?"

"Yeah. You know in a way you do."

"I think he looks exactly like him," the older policeman said.

In a tone of voice that confused Mr. Pescadoor—he wasn't sure if the man was teasing his buddy or just coming to the realization that Nick Pescadoor was Nick Pescadoor.

"Tell me," the younger one said, making a motion with his thumb to connect himself and his partner. "You think our wives'd like the sangria?"

"I don't see why not," Mr. Pescadoor said. He pulled his thick wallet out of his back pocket. Pulled out one of the cards of which, for just such occasions, he always kept a supply. He took his fountain pen out from the inside pocket of his sports coat. Went over to the corner of the porch where there was a flat surface to write on. "Finch and Dufek, right?" he called over to the men.

They smiled at one another, pleased to hear their names, pleased that he'd remembered them, pleased at the prospect of getting something for free. They nodded and said, "Yup," "Yes." Dufek, the younger one, spelled his name out to make sure Mr. Pescadoor didn't put a *c* before the *k*, as so many people did.

A successful businessman, Mr. Pescadoor knew how to make money on gifts. He did not put the men down on the card for free dinners, just all the sangria they and their wives could drink. "In any 24-hour period," he added for a light touch. He handed the card to Dufek, put away his pen and turned to go into the house.

As he stepped in the front door, Mrs. Lefferts was descending the staircase, her husband with his tools and her eldest daughter with the vacuum cleaner right behind her. The latter had heard Mr. Pescadoor's Jaguar pull into the drive and had gone upstairs to tell her mother.

"Joyce," Mr. Pescadoor said, raising both arms like an opera singer welcoming the diva back onto the stage to accept the audience's ovation.

Both at work and at home Mr. Pescadoor frequently made extravagant gestures of affection, and he relied on these to help customers, staff, friends and family feel he loved them without his having to use up his time talking with, or listening to, them. In this specific instance, he had not formulated any opinions against Mrs. Lefferts, or her family, but he did have a general policy on arriving home of trying to avoid or clear out any visitors who were not either part of his family or close friends of his family. He found it hard to relax with strangers around.

Mrs. Lefferts had decided, long ago, that Mr. Pescadoor was a not untypical, absolutely selfish, "successful" American male. Smiling away and being generous with his money and thinking therefore that he was a prince of a nice guy, on top of being a business whiz. While his daughter experimented with sex and mind-altering drugs; his youngest son grew more and more aloof and angry; and his wife descended through loneliness and lack of real work or stimulation to alcoholism. In response to Mr. Pescadoor's greeting she wrinkled her lips in a kind of half-smile, half-grimace. Reaching the bottom of the stairs she said, "You've come home," and looked away from Mr. Pescadoor. "Andrea, John, Elizabeth," she called to the rest of her family. "Mr. Pescadoor's returned, it's time for us to go. Get your coats on."

Mr. Pescadoor had stepped into the hall. Now he stepped forward again, shook hands and said hello to all the Lefferts gathered there. He looked over at all the broken, dirty things piled on the newspapers. Neatly separated, one type of item from the next. Pillows and towels stacked. The most damaged items—the pieces of them—in two large brown paper bags. "Quite a display," he said softly, half reflecting to himself, half remarking to the Lefferts group. He then noticed Knute who had come from the dining room with Andrea and was standing holding her hand, forming the left side of the Lefferts group. "Hi son," Mr. Pescadoor said and nodded at Knute. "Are you OK?"

Avoiding his father's eyes, Knute nodded, blushed a little. Then quickly ducked down, let go of Andrea's hand and slipped behind her, behind the Lefferts, and up onto the stairs. He sat down on the third step. Briefly unable to see or be seen by his father.

"It looks like a tornado passed through my bedroom," Mr. Pescadoor said. Then his eyes noted some pieces of his electric razor and he added, "And my bathroom."

"Forget your electric razor," Mrs. Lefferts said scornfully but under her breath so that Mr. Pescadoor understood only that she'd made a critical reply. "Come on family," she said. "It's past our bedtime."

The group said good-bye to Knute and his father, then moved around and ahead of her, through the hall and out the door onto the porch. Once all the others were safely out, Mrs. Lefferts stopped, in the doorway, and turned to Mr. Pescadoor. "I don't know if you had a good night at your restaurants," she said, her tone suggesting that she felt (as, making the most of the event, she did) great sadness.

Mr. Pescadoor shrugged. Of course, Friday night, that was the big night in his business. The big alcohol night. Mrs. Lefferts wanted him to do penance. He wanted her to go home.

She continued, "*They* had a rough night. They didn't do too well."

Mr. Pescadoor nodded, said softly, "So it seems. Unfortunately."

"Unfortunately. Very unfortunately," Mrs. Lefferts said. She pushed her hands into the pockets of her coat. Stared directly into Mr. Pescadoor's eyes. "Can I ask you a question?"

"Of course."

"What would happen to your business if you didn't go to work Friday nights?"

"In the short run?" Knute's father jiggled the keys and change in his pants pocket, attaching a sound to the casual mental reflection he was doing in his head.

"Short run, long run," Mrs. Lefferts said impatiently.

"In the short run, absolutely nothing. I have a very good staff. In the short run they could probably run my restaurants better than I do. But you know, Joyce—you know what the problem is in the long run?"

She shook her head, annoyed. She had asked a rhetorical question, she didn't want a considered answer.

"It's my money." He pressed his lips together, pulled his

eyebrows up, his expression suggesting, just a little, a clown's. A little sad, a little happy. "Even the best employee will only work so well for so long for someone else's profit if that someone else isn't there working just as hard or harder himself." He jingled his keys and change again, attaching a sound to the end of the idea.

Mr. Lefferts looked away, past Mr. Pescadoor to Knute on the stairs. "Nick," she said sadly. "It's obvious you're a very smart man. A marvelous restauranteur. I'm sure you already know that. And no one else doubts it or needs any more proof. The weaknesses lie in fatherdom."

She lowered her gaze to the red-tile entryway floor. Paused, letting things sink in. Then she looked back up, into Mr. Pescadoor's eyes. "I know that's quite a thing for one, fairly recent neighbor to say to another. But, you know, Nick—I've learned a few things in my life. And one of them is that, as a rule, *I'm* happier if I speak out instead of trying to hold my opinions in."

Her opinions were like split logs that stoked her own mental steam engine. "You've got a bad situation here in this house. You've got a middle-aged woman who hasn't had a husband— or a lover—in years. A twelve-year-old boy who's looking for a father."

Any interest Mr. Pescadoor might have had in talking with Mrs. Lefferts, he had lost. He was beginning to get very angry. But instead of his anger hardening him, causing him to raise his voice, it produced a smiling chumminess, a chumminess that could have been mistaken for great affection.

"Joyce," he said, smiling and stepping forward. He raised his left arm, intending to put it around her back, use it to turn her 180 degrees, so that she'd be facing the out-of-doors, the porch steps, the walk.

She stepped back onto the porch, still facing the house and out of range of his arm. "You think I'm just the neighborhood busybody, don't you? And the best thing to do is just gently shuffle me out, get me on my way."

Mr. Pescadoor nodded, kept smiling. "Joyce." He stepped forward again. A couple hundred of these steps and she'd have her back to *her own* front door. "You don't know how much I appreciate all you and your marvelous family have done for us Pescadoors tonight. We are truly blessed to have such wonderful neighbors. I mean it. When we went looking for this house, we were concerned that it be solidly built, big enough for all five of us, near the good schools—a lot of silly things it seems. Because I think what we've found—speaking for myself and Ginny especially—I think we've decided that this house's most important asset has to be you all, the Lefferts family. We feel extremely lucky, blessed. You people are saints. Maybe you don't believe me when I say this, but I mean it. You are a family of six saints. And I—"

"Nick," Mrs. Lefferts said sternly. A few compliments were to be expected, but a saint had to keep to the task at hand. "It all sounds very nice, you've got a golden tongue, Nick, but—"

"No, Joyce," he interrupted. And stepped forward again, again with his left arm out, trying to put it around her back. "I don't want you interrupting me when I'm trying to compliment you. You, and Henry—you are amazing parents. Four children—four times you went asking for trouble, right? But no, because you have raised wonderful children. . . . Which I think is a terrific tribute to your abilities as parents. Because— you may not believe that I know this, but I think I do—raising children is an art form. And not every parent, myself included, is born with the necessary talent. But—"

"But Nick—"

"No, Joyce, really—"

It was a good twenty minutes' work. And it wasn't a complete success. That is, Knute's father wasn't able to so completely dominate conversation that Mrs. Lefferts wasn't able to inflict him with a few more of her lines. Knute and his mother needed to "see more" of Mr. Pescadoor's "handsome face" and "bushy eyebrows." "I hope in my forthrightness I haven't overstepped the bounds of neighborliness. You'll forgive me if I have. . . . It doesn't have to be anything major, you know. One more night a week when you have dinner at home. A couple trips to the ballpark with Knute. Buy him a few hot dogs, give him a sip of your beer."

But. At the end. Mrs. Lefferts and family had retreated back to number 15 Oxford Street. Mr. Pescadoor had control of number 17.

He sighed with relief from the end of his walk as he waved his last wave to his marvelous neighbors. He felt like he used to in his nightclub days. Like a revolving door with a mouth. Clients, performers, staff, Mr. Bishop going in and out over and over again, him jabbering away with them all, until he was numb. Someone could whack him on the back with a stick, he wouldn't do more than blink his eyes once.

He turned, walked slowly up his walk, up his porch steps. Officers Finch and Dufek were still there, though they were making motions as if they had some intention of leaving. He went over and took their dishes; said good-bye. Left them on the lounger and went inside. Shut the front door. Took the coffee things into the kitchen and put them on the butcher block worktable there. Went over and patted Knute on the knee. "Some evening, eh?"

"I guess," Knute mumbled.

"You guess! I feel like somebody just tried to clean me on a washboard."

Knute looked at his sneakers and made a face. A slightly disgusted expression.

His father crouched down, looked at his son. "You and your mother had a fight?"

Knute nodded once, sharply. Gritted his teeth. Said nothing. Said nothing in a way that let his father know that he was saying nothing because he was angry. Mrs. Lefferts had said his father had "a twelve-year-old boy who's looking for a father." One of Knute's many sources of displeasure at that moment was the mingling in his memory of Mrs. Lefferts' opinions and the smile, warm laugh and soft blond hair of Mrs. Lefferts' daughter Andrea. It became the most accessible conclusion: It was all his father's fault. Knute hadn't yet realized quite what had happened, and he certainly hadn't wondered why the house-cleaning had been so much fun. But he knew it was all his father's fault.

Mr. Pescadoor watched the anger stiffening his son's features, glazing his eyes. He felt a little more tired. He was not a believer in getting to the root of emotions, airing conflicts. He preferred hoping the bad would pass quickly, urging it to; regularly reminding himself and those around him how well things were going.

He got up from his crouch. Stepped back away from the stairs. Looked around again at the muddy, broken things on the newspapers; on his other side the living room all lit up. He walked in there, switched off the two main lamps, went into the dining room and switched off the overhead lights there. Came back to the front hall. Turned again to Knute. "So what do we do now?" he asked. "Put some of this stuff away? Just go to bed? I think I'd like a Scotch on the rocks. You?" He laughed. "Can I make you anything? A ginger ale?"

Knute shook his head.

Mr. Pescadoor went into the kitchen to get a glass and some ice. Knute got up, went over to the newspapers, the pile of possessions. Started first with the clothes and linens. Those had to be put in the washing machine right away, he thought. And he started gathering them up, yanking the pillow cases off the pillows, making three piles—lights, darks, colors.

As he became more physically active, his mind also started working harder. Concentrating on his father. What was he doing making himself a drink when there was so much work to be done! He'd just gotten home, he [Knute] had been home all evening dealing with his mother. But of course his father didn't know how to do laundry. He was too busy with his restaurants to even know how to run a washing machine. Or how to fix a window like Mr. Lefferts did. A lot of kids' fathers could do stuff like that. And they'd have their kids do projects

123

with them on weekends, show them how to use tools and things. He just had his mother and painting and gardening and skating all the time. . . .

His father, drink prepared, briefly interrupted this thinking by coming into the hall again, asking how he could help.

"Just go to bed," Knute said, almost breaking into tears.

His father sat down on the stairs. "Take it easy, kiddo," he said. "We can do laundry in the morning. Why don't you come sit here with me a sec?"

Yeah right, and leave all this water soaking through the newspapers and onto the floor all night. Knute didn't look over at his father. He shook his head, gathered up the largest of his three laundry piles, headed into the kitchen, then down to the basement.

For the next half-hour or so his father stayed in the hall, sitting on the stairs, sipping his drink. Staying up until his son was ready to go to bed, wondering if he could come to any clear, useful thoughts about why this one Friday night fight, which Mrs. Lefferts and Knute had taken so seriously, was actually serious.

As far as he knew, Knute and his mother were thick as thieves. They went skating together, swimming, trips. It seemed to him the two of them got along better, were closer than probably any other pairing in the family, he and his wife included. . . .

His thoughts drifted off. Then came back. So. So, so. So something had led to a fight. It seemed only to be expected when a mother and son were very close. It went with the territory.

He and his mother had had some terrible yelling fights. She'd thrown things at him. He still had a scar on his temple just under his hair from the time his mother had hit him with the saucer of a coffee cup. But they'd also cried together afterward, her tears wetting his hair, his blood wetting the front of her blouse. People in the neighborhood often used to remark on what a team they were, how close they seemed to be.

He sipped some more of his Scotch. Watched blankly for a while as Knute worked away on the piles of broken possessions.

It wasn't like Knute to be working so determinedly, he thought. That was more Nick Jr.'s style. He'd thought Knute was more the thoughtful, philosophical type.

Like his father? No, he laughed to himself. He [Nick] was more a plodder. Or a hanger-on. He just hung on and hung on, fiddling with whatever seemed to need fiddling with, whatever no one else was fiddling with. Chatting away, smiling at people, keeping things calm, running in their channels.

And the dollars kept running in their channel. That was a kind of miracle, he decided. A miracle almost in the religious sense. . . .

He started wondering about perhaps, when he was older and his kids were all settled in careers, marriages, maybe he'd start giving most of his income away. To help foster-children. Or maybe scholarships for inner-city kids, so they could study unusual things, like art history, archaeology . . .

Chapter 4

The next morning Mrs. Pescadoor began joking about their fight. "This year we just decided to do our spring cleaning early—and to do a very thorough job. Right? . . . What's one TV more or less?"

For many years Knute disassociated himself from the fight. It wasn't an event he had been involved in, it was a story his mother liked to tell and of which one of the main characters happened to share his name. He would wince when his mother would begin telling the story to someone. He felt he was wincing out of embarrassment for his mother because she was telling this stupid story yet again, and because she didn't realize she'd already told it to this particular person at least once.

When Knute was at college, more than 500 miles from home, he began to cherish his memory of the fight (or his memory of the fight as it had evolved listening to his mother's evolving story of the fight). It wasn't that back then, twelve years old, he'd stood up to his mother; it was the unusualness of the event he cherished. It gave him an opportunity to imagine that he, and his mother, were different, perhaps special or unique. Millions of males and females had been born in the same year as him, they'd grown up in suburbs outside American cities, been classified in the same percentile of college entrance examinees. Right there at his college were two thousand kids who shared his background. But had *any of them* ever gotten in such a fight? Only a few of Knute's college friends had, at least as far as he knew. And even with them, the stories, the details of their fights—or acts of vandalism, burglary, pyromania—were, necessarily, different. And Knute avoided asking his friends to tell him their stories, and tried not to pay attention when they told them anyway.

*

Intermittently throughout Knute's childhood and his adulthood he would, does and will get carried away as he did during his fight with his mother and in breaking Toni's arm. In terms of time, these incidents will make up an insignificant fraction of Knute's life; but being dramatic, singular and emotional, they have, or are going to have, a significant place in his memory. And their drama and singularity, the feelings they have unleashed have given them a significant place in this novel. In fact, although this was not my original intention, the weight that is this book is now supported by four such dramatic incidents—by the four most dramatic incidents I imagined having taken place between when Knute entered the fourth grade and when he finished the ninth. But by and large Knute's life was not and is not notably dramatic; and, again and of course, the record of his childhood is made up of much more than just these incidents.

*

Knute's birth, from the obstetrician's point of view, was routine, or perhaps a little simpler than usual. For Mrs. Pescadoor more was involved, and she announced afterward that as far as she could make out what all her children had done was wait until she had no more energy left to be enthusiastic about their arrival—then they "arrove." Knute was her third child though. The other two had taken longer, she had known less what to expect, been less sure that an end would come eventually, been very frightened at times. With number three—she was a pro, exhausted as she was at the end.

Not so for Knute. Among so many other things: It was only after he had lived in the air many million or more times longer that he was able to begin to understand that he had absolutely no memory of his first moments, his first months, years even. And he never was going to have any such memories.

Which didn't stem his fantasies, emotions, jokes.

After graduating from college Knute moved all the way west and got an apartment one block from the Pacific. The first winter living there he worked nights as a limousine driver. Sometimes it was dawn when he went to bed; he rarely woke up before eleven, and from then, till noon or one, he would often stay in his bed, thinking, dozing, dreaming, reflecting, staring at the ceiling or at the little hills and river valleys his covers formed at the foot of the bed, listening to the groups going by under his window, on their way to or from the beach.

Had it really been better in the womb? he wondered one day. Yes of course, he quickly decided. You had to be kidding yourself to pretend it hadn't. Hooked right up to Mom, floating in warm fluids, excreting at will.

He smiled. He felt good just thinking about it, moving his bare legs under the sheet.

On another day he wondered if it wasn't a kind of slavery, or imprisonment. His father getting his dark, thick penis between his mother's thighs and up into her vagina. His father's sperm getting to her ovum. And then—at least in the U.S. of A., after the first trimester—it was all over.

The pain of labor. His overlarge head trying to get back the other way, through his mother's vagina. The sheer work of it. And the work of living.

And all the times he—and his mother too, he assumed— just wanted to say no, I quit. No hard feelings, but I am going to fall off this balcony (if you can assure me there's no danger of ending up a quadriplegic, with overwhelming medical bills and no hope of a normal adult sex life. Whatever that might be.)

For ten years beginning when he was twenty-four, Knute was involved with a woman named Martha; for eight of those years they were husband and wife. Martha got to hear a lot about Knute's childhood. There was one period when he was trying, evenings in the bathtub, to visualize his birth. "I've been able to get the components," he said. "White sheet, female crotch, lots of blood, a hairless head—but the images are always vague. Plus, the baby doesn't have any of my features; I think it must be a kid I saw in one of those magazine articles on the miracle of birth.

"The crotch belongs to a girl I saw in a different kind of magazine. She would have been an Olympic gymnast if at age ten she hadn't developed breasts the size of hot air balloons. So now she just does handstands with her ten boyfriends on the beach. And then goes home to take her clothes off."

With the less visceral circumstances of his birth Knute's imagination was more productive. He had a sense of a large room, in an isolated wing of a very quiet, if not otherwise empty, hospital. The room large enough for a dozen or more beds, but containing only one. Everything brand-new, brightly lit. White walls; high, white ceiling; white cabinets with glass fronts.

The bed stainless steel. His mother just a motionless white sheet that peaked where her knees might be raised. The doctor and the nurse faceless—two sets of hands; the latter's female, thin and pinkish fingers; the doctor's male, broad and thick, black hair covering the back sides.

Knute told Martha the lights had been too bright. The lights had been too bright, the walls too white, the doctor's hands too cold, his mother too drugged. The circumstances of his delivery had been too cold and institutional, and therefore, he maintained, as an adult he suffered from constipation, premature balding, he had trouble talking to women in bathing suits.

Starting before he met Martha, long before they decided to have children, Knute developed the habit of going to public libraries and reading books on human reproduction and child-care. He told Martha he believed it was one of a fertile adult's primary responsibilities: to inform him or herself about these subjects. After she became pregnant with the first of their two daughters, Knute interviewed a dozen doctors and midwives and toured delivery rooms in their city. The room he chose had unfinished wood paneling, recessed lighting and a tub in which the father could bathe with his newborn child.

One Saturday morning not long before they decided to get married, they were driving to a country inn where they were going to spend the weekend. They were discussing the possi-bility of getting married, having children. All of a sudden, as if angry, Knute swerved onto the shoulder of the road, stopped and turned off the car. He wanted Martha to realize how seri-ous he was—if they had male children they were not going to be circumcised.

Martha raised her eyebrows and looked sideways at him, amused by how worked up he was about the subject. She came from a Jewish family and circumcision was by that time stan-dard for Americans, Jews and Gentiles alike. But, as she told Knute: "It really doesn't matter to me one way or another. I hereby leave any foreskin of any of our sons entirely in your hands."

After Martha became pregnant with their first child, Knute again made a stern pronouncement against circumcision and Martha again said it made no difference to her. Nonetheless, throughout the pregnancy, Knute wouldn't let go of the subject. "They'll have to castrate me before they circumcise any son of mine!" "Everybody claims it's for health reasons—it's just barbaric. It's a barbaric custom we've inherited from primitive societies." "Do they cut off people's toes so they don't get athlete's foot? Or what about baby girls' labia? You want a nice breeding ground for bacteria and disease—all those little folds of skin, kept so warm and moist—there isn't a better place on earth for bacteria. But does that mean you take a scalpel and start hacking away?"

"Three days old or whatever I was—they don't wait till the kid is old enough to have his own opinion about what condition he wants his penis to be in." "The foreskin is the most sensitive part of the male anatomy. Essentially, before I was a week old they had removed half my capacity to experience sexual pleasure."

The winter of his sophomore year of college, Knute had spent a lot of his time following around two juniors majoring in philosophy. Hegel, the *nun* (a Greek word), Wittgenstein, the Apollonian and the Dionysian, and on and on, epistemology—they mentioned a lot of things in their dialogues. Knute was mainly left with the (quite inaccurate) feeling that even if he only studied European languages and read philosophy texts for the rest of his life, he still wouldn't know half as much as his two friends did. But he also retained a few ideas, suggestions; including the possibility that knowledge and words were inextricably linked. He might not have known anything before he had known words or phrases for things. The world is an idea, in Kant's (translated) phrase.

Lying in his bed by the Pacific one afternoon, Knute recalled this idea, and he wondered about himself just hours, days old, in his hospital crib. His flesh held in a bundle by his skin and the blankets. But not knowing there was any object—close or far away—that was flesh. And separate things that were skin, blanket, crib, invisible air, light. Expressions appearing on his face or in his limbs. People—nurses, relatives—leaning over him, studying all these expressions. Drawing conclusions. He's feeling this or that. Above him lips, heads moving in conversation. Or to make more expressions. For the thing in the crib.

And they'd decided that he wanted thus or so. And thus or so had been given or taken away from him. Sometimes for the better, sometimes for the worse.

What had he known/did he know? He was like a cloud. A cloud that was sometimes dissipating, sometimes contracting. And as it dissipated parts of him would feel very relaxed and other parts afraid. As it contracted he felt uncomfortable, and stronger!

When he and his mother were ready to go home from the hospital, his father, brother and sister all came in the lime green Lincoln his father was driving at that time. There was a bit of a quarrel outside on the street because his sister wanted to hold him in the car, but his mother said she would prefer to hold him herself. He was such a little baby. She told his sister it was very important to be careful with him, particularly when going places in the car.

At his father's urging a compromise was reached. His sister sat in the middle of the front seat with him (Knute) on her lap and both hands holding him tight to her abdomen. On her right sat his mother, one arm also holding him in his sister's lap, the other arm on his sister's shoulder. His dad, on the left, drove but kept his right hand on the pile of Knute, blanket and hands.

"When I was growing up," Knute told Martha, "everyone—my mother, my father, my sister, brother—used to tell me all the time about all this work that had been done to prepare for my birth and when I came home. They built a room in the attic for my sister, that was the major effort. Plus they expanded the bathroom so there'd be space for a changing table. I got my sister's old room, which was the room the bathroom had been expanded into. We moved to the house we have now when I was in the third or fourth grade, so I don't remember the first one that well . . .

"Apparently, I spent my first three years surrounded by zoo animals and scenery. Anne claims she tried to dissuade her, but my mother insisted on putting up this wallpaper with these big tigers, lions, elephants, palm trees . . .

"Anne bought me an African violet. When my mother and I were still at the hospital she and my father were shopping at the supermarket and there were these plants on the floor there. You know how they have plants in supermarkets, in those green plastic pots? And the plants usually look plastic, or else they're dying from insufficient light and because it's too drafty on the floor. According to my brother, my sister decided she and my father should buy me the most pitiful plant in the whole store. Because—like me—it needed a home, tender, loving care.

"It died almost instantly—according to my brother. It was sick to begin with and then Anne flooded it with water and put it next to my crib where there was no direct sun. It rotted. My brother says about six months later my mother finally noticed there was this moldy thing in a pot next to my crib and she took it out to the garage . . .

"You want to know what my brother's like? Remember, he's the one who told me this story—twenty times at least. He says on the Fourth of July—my first Fourth of July—to help me celebrate my total dependence, he dumped the dirt out of the pot, put a couple M–8os under it, and blew the thing into a million pieces."

"He's always loved his fireworks, my brother. I remember when I was kid he used to always want to take me out to the garage to show me his stocks. He sold fireworks through the mail—I think he still does. A little illegal business he could amuse himself with. He used to make me come with him to the park, or out to the sandbox that was supposedly for my nephew and niece to play in. My brother liked to use it to demonstrate his latest wares.

"I don't know. It's always seemed to me that life itself is

anxiety-provoking enough—without having to go playing around with firecrackers, or play around with selling them illegally through the mails.

"I guess it seemed to Nick that his little brother was a chicken. I'll bet you over a dozen times in that garage he told me how I'd better be careful not to grow up to be a faggot. He had some great lines. He only had one younger brother, he sure as hell didn't ever want to find out he was going around swallowing other guys' come. . . . I remember once he gave me this long rap on how guys were going to come up to me in the locker room at the high school and propose doing perverse things with me. I was supposed to refuse them.

"I used to just sit down on the floor of the garage and lean against the wall. Think about about playing the organ or the homework I had to do. Wait for my sister-in-law to call us for dinner."

"Supposedly, starting when I was around six months old, I began having trouble swallowing. Not all the time, just occasionally some bit of food—or milk—would get caught in the back of my throat, I'd choke on it and have trouble breathing.

"According to the doctor, the thing itself that caused the choking wasn't serious. It was just some piece of flesh in the back of my throat that had grown too fast or too slowly. But the consequences were truly dangerous. My mother has told me that on a couple occasions she had to rush me to the hospital, to get them to give me oxygen. She used to put me in the car with all the windows open and drive as fast as she could around the neighborhood to get me air.

"I don't remember a minute of it. She says a couple times I turned blue. I have no memory of being blue."

Knute was a very slow eater. By the time he was in college it had become a vanity of his. Going through the cafeteria line he would overload his tray with saucers and dishes of food—two vegetables, bread, fruit, cake, milk, water. Then at the table he'd pick—jab his fork into the cake and pull off a small mouthful. Then pause, look around the room, or look at those with whom he was sitting, to ascertain if his mannerisms were drawing at least a little attention. He'd saw off a bit of his chicken, poke that in his mouth. Another pause and survey of the room. Then maybe three green beans, one for each tine of the fork.

This performance was best suited to cafeteria-style service and the captive and familiar audience a college dining hall provides. But Knute had been eating this way long before he went to college, and he continued afterward. And, when Martha would tease him about it, saying it looked ridiculously affected and one day soon would surely cease to be amusing—and become boring—Knute protested that it wasn't an act. It was a result of the medical problems he'd experienced in infancy. Even though he could swallow without risk now, subconsciously (he claimed) he retained a memory of choking himself, being always on the verge of self-strangulation.

"You have no memory of doing anything with your father," Martha said once. "He was just a traveling salesman who spent the occasional night with your mother. She just told you he was your father and they were married so you wouldn't feel ashamed at school. Those stories about your dad and the Navy—what you were supposed to realize is the guy's still in the Navy, fathering Pescadoors in every port of call."

Knute laughed. "I do have memories of my father. I remember seeing his picture in the newspaper—in ads for his restaurants. He was a very happy man—always smiling."

Knute was never really much of a smoker. In college he got up to as many as a dozen a day. When he was with Martha and she was still smoking he'd bum a few a day from her. He liked the idea of smoking, the image—of a nervous, intense person. He'd suck hard on his cigarettes and wave them around as if he couldn't keep his hands still.

This afternoon, after trading jokes with Martha about his father, he fished a cigarette out of her pack, lit it, sucked on it, leaned back in his chair, then leaned forward quickly, both elbows on the table, his shoulders pushing up around his long, skinny neck. "I can remember sometimes on Sunday mornings we'd wait hours for him to wake up and have breakfast with us. I'd go in the basement and play the organ or something. My mother and I wouldn't eat a thing until my father came down, ready to eat with us. I don't know why not. I don't remember feeling hungry or getting annoyed.

"I used to ask him if we could wash his car. Seriously. He's always had beautiful cars, he gets a new one every year. I don't know why, but when I was a kid I always wanted to wash them.

"He had this man at a garage in the city who he paid to keep his cars clean. But whenever I asked he'd always say yes, and he'd get up, bring his newspaper, or a cigar, and come sit on the front steps and watch me washing away."

Knute's hand darted over the ashtray and with his long bony index finger he gave the cigarette a tap. Then he took another hard drag and started speaking again, louder and enunciating carefully, like a professor who'd come to the point in the lecture that he wanted to make sure his students recorded in their notes.

"My father is a genius. There is just no question that in his area, the type of business he's in, he is a genius.

"My grandfather was able to save absolutely no money. Every penny he earned he spent the week he earned it. And not because he was wasteful; he had a big family, he didn't earn much money.

"By the time my father was sixteen he was earning as much as my grandfather. He was the assistant manager at a bowling alley. Even at sixteen years old, a poor Italian kid, they recognized how capable he was. He just had—and he still has—an innate sense of exactly the right way to run a service business—supervise staff, coordinate supplies, get along with customers.

"In sixty years he's gone from zero to a couple million. (I happen to know he has at least that much.) That's a couple million *after* putting his brothers and one sister and his children through college and supporting his parents in their old age. And he started with absolutely no capital. If you ask me, that's an incredible achievement. It just takes more nerve, and more hope, than most people have. More than I can ever imagine having. Plus it takes the authority to tell other people what to do, to get banks to lend you money when you have nothing to offer except your self-possession and the ability to talk a good line.

"I just have a tremendous respect for what he's done. The money is irrelevant; it's the ambition and the achievement."

Chapter 5

My father is a professor of history, my mother a psychiatric social worker. I was born in 1954 in Boston. I lived in Cambridge until I was eight, then in St. Louis for four years and then in Ann Arbor, Michigan, until 1971, when I went off to college.

In June 1976, I graduated from the University of California at Berkeley and moved to New York City. For a week I camped out in the living room of some California friends' apartment. Then an old Ann Arbor friend invited me to come stay where he was staying in a large apartment on Broadway between 106th and 107th streets. It belonged to a widowed schoolteacher who was traveling that summer in Israel, and with whose eldest daughter "Marcello"—my friend—was sleeping.

Any other kids were away, so there was plenty of room for me. Plus, in the living room, a grand piano on which I wrote a few tunes which I remember at the time fancying were very

(Duke) Ellingtonian. Though the fact is I cannot play the piano.

But Marcello and I did used to jam away for hours—me on the piano, him on bongo drums (which he could play). The living room was large and got a lot of light. Behind me, as I sat at the piano, were large windows that looked out over the tops of the trees of this little park there on Broadway. Very nice. (The ideal way to look for your first job in New York.)

Across Broadway there was (and still is, I believe) a restaurant called The Balcony. It was built out a little onto the sidewalk, and there was a row or two of tables there; in good weather separated from the people walking on the sidewalk only by some wood framing. (That is, the framing for the windows that would be closed in bad weather.) Very pleasant. Very European, we imagined. (We were young.) We would order things like Pernod, Campari, and sit there in the late afternoons entertaining ourselves with sophisticated opinions on culture, philosophy, women.

From where Marcello and I liked to sit we could see 107th Street—right along the block and beyond, to the trees of Riverside Park. And it so happened that in late June there we were able to watch one of the more wonderful natural phenomena of New York City—the setting of the sun (a fat, simmering, yellow disk)—right between the buildings on either side of a crosstown street.

But can this rite be observed once a year (per street) or twice? That is the question. That was the question about which Marcello and I chose to get in a tremendous, multi-day argument. (Not our first such argument of course.)

It threatened to ruin my living arrangement plus force Marcello to spend more of his time with this schoolteacher's daughter whose charms perhaps did not go much beyond the bedroom (or at least the bedroom plus no rent plus grand piano, et cetera).

Marcello said once a year. Why, I can't remember. I said twice. Obviously. Things with the sun happen twice a year. E.g., the equinoxes, solstices. (But, perhaps Marcello argued, not summer and winter. Yes, there are two solstices, but one ushers in a very hot season, the other a very cold one.)

Neither of us knew anything about astronomy beyond what we'd been taught by the same junior high school science teachers and an odd fact or two we'd picked up from the *New York Times*. Which doesn't mean we alternated arguing with trips to the library or telephone calls to friends who *had* studied astronomy. Nor can I remember either one of us ever saying there was any area of the subject about which we weren't fully informed. (Kant—as either one of us philosophy amateurs may point out during the next argument—was adamant about his disinterest in the physiology of thought.)

We drew diagrams on the cocktail napkins of how the earth and sun related to one another. All the diagrams were exactly right, according to the diagrammers. His were just completely different from mine. And he couldn't believe—it wasn't a question of science or the sun and New York—but, he was just curious: Was I really so sure of myself I couldn't ever even consider the possibility that someone else might know more about a given subject than I did?

Oh, Marcello—do you even listen to what comes out of

your mouth! What could be more arrogant than getting all em-
broiled in a stupid argument about the sun because you mis-
spoke once about the number of times it set in a particular way
and then attacked the character of the person who—just by
chance perhaps—happened to know the right answer?

Et cetera. Just before the argument short-circuited our
friendship, one of us suggested we write a play. About two
young men arguing about how many times the sun set right
between the buildings of the crosstown streets of Manhat-
tan . . .

We set up two typewriters on either end of the table in the
schoolteacher's dining room. (A large, dark brown, oval table
which filled almost all of a narrow, dark room.) We sat down
behind the machines. Turned in the first sheets of paper. One
of us, I can't remember which, was to type all Marcello's
lines, the other all of mine.

But. First we had to have names. Pseudonymns. What
should they be?

Marcello knew exactly. The way he presented it, it was as if
he'd always known—there could be no question, these were
our names. For him, Marcello (as in Marcello Mastroianni,
one of our screen idols). (The young man's real name is just a
short, four-letter name. Not uncommon in America—or in
Scandinavia. Though "Marcello" generally goes by a diminutive and has chosen to spell that diminutive in a slightly unusual way.)

For me, yes, Knute.

I don't remember being more than a little taken aback at the
time. (And, in one sense, the name wasn't very significant

since we only worked two afternoons on the play, never got beyond establishing the setting, never got back to the argument.) I do remember thinking, though, when I found myself using the name Knute for the protagonist of the short story that has evolved into this novel, that somehow I was getting back at Marcello. Turning the tables, deflecting the joke off me and onto him. Why, I now have no idea.

*

When Knute was growing up, in June and July before they went to his grandparents' cabin, his mother used to take him to a lake that was not far from their town. It was a man-made lake, Army Corps of Engineers–made. Small, peanut-shaped. Most of the land surrounding the shore had not been cleared. There were a few private cabins among the trees, and a landing where people could put in boats.

The beach section was on a steep slope that had been cleared of all but a few young trees and then planted in grass. At the top of the hill was the parking lot, the ticket-seller, the snack bar and the bathrooms/changing rooms. A concrete path with an iron guardrail wound down across the lawn to a low concrete retaining wall. Beyond the wall was a dock and a four- or five-foot strip of sandy beach.

The beach users spread their towels on the lawn, the different groups—teenagers, families, elderly couples—claiming different regions. Mrs. Pescadoor liked to set up in the middle of the teenagers, almost all the way down the slope near where the dock began. She knew most all the kids' names, and as she and Knute made their way to the area she'd selected she would

call, "Hello, Mikey! Hello, Mary, Candy!"—greeting everyone she approached. Most of the kids would nod politely in
response; a few of the girls would get excited by the little boy,
Knute: "Gonna go swimming with me today, Knute? You better—'member how you promised me yesterday?" "Bring your
pail today?" "Will you catch a big fish for me today, Knute?"

According to his mother's schedule, on arrival they would
spread their towels and go down to the shore to go swimming.
His mother would work with him on his swimming for ten or
fifteen minutes, and then on her own she would swim out beyond the floats defining the public swimming area. Knute
would sit on the bank watching her, her long arms sweeping
into the water, a flutter of bubbles at her heels, as she moved
out of sight to the far corner of the lake and then came back
again. Next was lunch, then a few hours of tanning, listening
to the kids' radios and their giggling, discussing, flirting.

Mrs. Pescadoor was very proud of her back dive and would
try to get the teenage boys interested in watching her practice
it or, better, to let her try and teach it to them. A few of the
girls, more out of pity than interest, did come down to the dock
and take instruction. And some of the boys would occasionally
pretend they were trying to learn the dive and would draw a
laugh from their friends by doing a theoretically mock-graceful
version of Mrs. Pescadoor's dive, ending up making a loud
splat and a big splash.

Knute did usually bring his plastic pail and his plastic
shovel. He would walk around, knee- to waist-deep in the
water, trying to shovel minnows into the pail, or to drive them
up onto the sand, or split up the schools by stepping right into
them, or falling onto them, dumping water on them. With the

146

warmth of the sun, the cool water, other people talking, yelling, the fish twisting and turning, dividing and regrouping, it
was like swimming inside a kaleidoscope.

Along one edge of the lake was a small concrete dam over
the top of which ran a single railroad track, a spur leading from
a quarry to a freight depot. Very rarely did trains pass, but
people used the track for walking from one side of the lake to
the other. At least for a child, or an especially thin adult, the
traverse was a little dangerous because it included a segment
in which in the middle of the track there was nothing between
the ties but the sheer wall of the dam and the rocky stream,
broken bottles and rusting cans below.

For Knute, crossing the dam offered even more excitement
because, in order to get to the railroad track from the beach,
he had to walk past a part of the shore that was overgrown with
plants, some of which he had decided were poison sumac. At
his grandparents' cabin one time, his brother had identified a
stand of plants as poison sumac and had described to Knute
how once camping with some friends he had fallen naked into
such a stand and it had been a week before he could wear
underwear again. It seemed to the ten-, eleven-year-old Knute
to be a necessary test of toughness, getting poison sumac on
one's penis and not being able to wear underwear therefore.
But he never got it, not at his grandparents' and not at this
lake. (In spite of his and his brother's imaginations, there were
no stands of poison sumac at either location, and for his part
Knute always kept his distance from the plants he had erro-
neously identified.)

It was a major part of his lake experience though. Asking

his mother if he could walk out to the dam; half hoping she'd say no, but knowing she almost always said yes. Asking if she'd watch his pail and shovel, he didn't want any of the other kids using it (and he wanted to prolong the discussion rather than begin the terrible trek). Asking if his mother would be there when he got back? Was she going for another swim? Was she going to watch him?

Finally, setting out. Across the grass and down to the concrete wall and walking along it and then hopping down onto the sand, then into the water so he could sneak around the poison sumac, and up the path out of his mother's sight, up the gravel bank to the tracks; while there was still gravel between the ties, practicing to get his stride perfectly measured for the distance between those ties, his feet sticking on the brown-black creosote; back into his mother's line of sight, not looking up though, concentrating on the ties, hearing people going by, then the sound of the water trickling through the slit at the top of the dam and then the view—nothing—air, water, rocks far below—he'd feel dizzy, high, queasy; his breath would catch in his throat and he'd have to turn around very carefully, like a tightrope walker turning on the high wire, except with the sound of water slipping down the concrete, and he could only hope that he would one day make it back to his towel next to his mother's towel; his mother; all the girls who knew his name and wanted to take his hand and play in the sand with him.

*

One day lying in his bed by the Pacific Knute tried to determine what his earliest memory was. The smell, or feel, of the basement laundry room in their first house? The washer and dryer making it so warm and humid. He had a sense of dimness, grayness. His mother never turning on the lights (though of course she normally did turn on the lights). Perhaps it was just when he went down alone that he left the lights off. In the late afternoons after school, or Saturday mornings. Only a little daylight coming in the cellar windows; that looked out on a lower part of the dull-silver-colored, intertwined, twisted wire driveway fence. The dead twigs and branches and tiny leaves of the bushes on the neighbors' side. The daylight sitting on the shiny gray of the ironing board, or covering a pile of towels his mother had left there.

Knute and his mother drove a lot of miles together. Back and forth to Florida. Back and forth to his grandparents'. In and out of the city hundreds of times.

As usual Mrs. Pescadoor had her systems. If they were driving west, she'd have the desk clerk at the motel wake them at five; they'd drive until around three when the glare began to bother her. Then they'd spend the rest of the afternoon at the pool of the next motel. Driving east they'd get up late and have a leisurely breakfast, then drive until it got dark. They had two thermoses, one for Mrs. Pescadoor's coffee, the other for Knute's apple juice, or whatever he felt like having to drink. Bags of peanuts, cheese and crackers. Knute's job was to prepare his mother food and drink when she wanted it, to navigate and to pick the motels and restaurants. Mrs. Pescadoor was in charge of driving and the radio.

From his Pacific bed he could remember the sweet drowsiness produced by sun and carbon monoxide. His head bumping against the window when he was falling asleep. Big trucks roaring past, making the station wagon sway. Blue metal silos standing up in the fields, and fading signs painted on the sides of old barns—caves ahead, jungle animals, pralines. Trains running along by the side. All the different names—Illinois Central, Santa Fe, Burlington Northern, Union Pacific. The Rock Island Line. Counting the cars, not counting the cars; trying to find license plates from all the different states. A mirage on a slight rise in the highway. Heat waves. Corn fields and green plants that his mother always told him were soybeans no matter what they looked like. Piles of coal, quarries and feed mills. The curving acres of browning fields and whitening sky. Green signs spanning the highway as cities approached, routes divided. In the early morning the gray light, mists, sometimes very heavy, so he just saw a yellow-gray-white, car lights. Later in the day the sun struck his face, and there were station wagons with children sitting in the way-backs waving at him. Laughing about something that might have to do with him or his mother or their station wagon; probably didn't. Between him and their laughing and jumping about plates of safety glass and the space above the highway, all of them speeding farther and farther ahead.

In winter going out to the ponds to skate with his mother. In the late afternoon. When the sky got gray. It seemed gray was the favorite color of his memory. The white-gray of winter. With maybe just a pulse of purple or rose to the west, from the sunset. The branches of the trees brittle, thin. Everything so quiet. Just the voice of his mother. Very clear from across the pond. "You better be careful over here, Knute, there's a huge crack!" Or his sister and a friend skating arm in arm singing the Hallelujah Chorus or whatever—music they sang in school.

His mother racing him. Cut, cut, cut, cut; the sound of the metal pushing off the ice. Perhaps he had given up skating essentially when he had gotten old enough to beat his mother. Perhaps he could have beaten her when he was younger if his hearing hadn't been as good as it was, or his mother's had been better. He had been lost in the sounds of the wind blowing through the trees, creaking trunks, shifting ice, crows. His mother had been down there concentrating—"On your mark, get set, go!"

Now, living on the West Coast where ponds never freeze and people skate on pavement, on wheels, it has become precious to him, the rasping sound of skates pushing against ice. He and his mother sucking in the cold air, panting; her little cries as she fought and got ahead of him. Her laughing happily, waiting for him at the finish.

Going back home in the car, his mother would tell him and his sister what great kids they were. How much fun she had with them. Or had just with him if his sister wasn't along. What a perfect child he was. Not always fighting with his mother, able just to have a good time with her, be her friend.

He remembers his mother once telling him and Anne that each of her children had a separate and distinct personality the

day he or she was born. And—it was implicit in her remark—
she knew what the personality was. But he can't remember her
ever saying what those personalities were.

He has developed his own theory. Which is that obstetricians
should figure out a way, perhaps it would be some kind of
injection, which can brief infants—before birth—on what
kind of mothers they have. Perhaps this potion could somehow
collect the opinions of a mother's friends, her husband, maybe
her boss at work if she worked, the neighbors. A range of
opinion. (And there could be another injection to brief the kid
on his father.) But that way the kid wouldn't have to spend
years finding out, say, that his mother was stubborn as hell. Or
not much of a listener. That her advice was more well inten-
tioned than sound.

Playing the organ. One year before he was born his mother
had bought an organ complete with all sorts of gadgets. It
could lay down various beats for you, provide a bass line, fill
in various chords when you played just a single note. His
mother rarely played it, and the organ was moved to the basement, where, by the time he was twelve, Knute was going
regularly, playing hour upon hour.

Sometimes he'd "improvise," using the gadgets, singing
every word that came into his head while he played all the
notes he could get his fingers on. He also bought the sheet
music for pop songs he heard on the radio and learned to play
them. And sometimes Anne would come down and show him
classical scales to practice, or she'd give him some of her easier music to work on.

It seemed to Knute like every day his mother would make at least one appearance. Come down, stand behind him at the bench and put her hand on his shoulder. "What's the song? Maybe I can sing along." It was a good fifteen minutes' work convincing her no, he didn't want her singing along, or sitting on the couch and listening, or going in the laundry room to catch up on her ironing. Sometimes he'd have to turn off the organ, go upstairs and out to the garage, get his bike and ride around the neighborhood for a half-hour or so. Then he could slip back into the house and down to the basement and go back to his practicing.

*

Every winter an ice show came to the arena in the city. Mrs. Pescadoor, seeing the ad for the show in the papers, would fill out the coupon and send off a check for, say, a dozen tickets. Nick Sr. was always too busy to go, and Nick Jr. would refuse, saying he hated ice shows and figure-skating. Mrs. Pescadoor would announce gaily to Knute and Anne—"I think we're gonna have plenty of extra tickets, you can invite your friends."

Anne would find a friend to go with her. Knute would try half-heartedly, but he felt embarrassed asking kids in his class—who liked ice *hockey*—to come see figure-skating and clowns. He never got anyone to come, though one time Mrs. Pescadoor convinced Doug to join them.

Mrs. Pescadoor was not embarrassed by ice shows or by having to ask people to come with her family to see them.

She'd ask the mother of the girl who took piano lessons right after Anne. Perhaps her daughter wanted to come? She didn't know if she and Anne were friends, maybe not—but they *should* be friends, they both liked to play the piano. Maybe the mother wanted to come too? She had plenty of tickets. Good seats, she'd ordered the first day, she always did. She loved ice shows. She thought it was the most beautiful thing, figure skating. *When* it was done well. Now some shows, some skaters, in her opinion . . .

She'd ask her "good buddy," as she called one of the pharmacists at a local drugstore. His wife had died of cancer shortly after the Pescadoors had moved to the suburb. He hadn't remarried, because—Mrs. Pescadoor first decided—he was too sweet and timid to ask women out on dates. She used to invite him every year to come and have Thanksgiving dinner with her and her family, and every year he'd decline politely, saying he'd already promised this or that one of his children or one of his friends. Then one year he said he'd come, and asked if he could bring "a friend" with him. Mrs. Pescadoor told him, "Sure, by all means, the more the merrier." But then later, when she and Knute and Anne were doing the clean-up, she said she was "a little annoyed with" the pharmacist, she felt "taken advantage of. . . . One extra person for Thanksgiving dinner is no big deal—I've still gotta cook the turkey. But I don't want to turn one of our few nice, relaxed family occasions into a computer dating service. The two of them sit right next to each other—hardly even look at anyone else at the table. I mean—"

"You did seat them next to each other," Anne interrupted.

"That's not the point. She's twenty-five years younger than him for God's sake!"

The pharmacist never wanted to go see the show. Sometimes the paperboy and his younger sister would go along. Often one or both of Knute's female cousins (Bridget's daughters) would come, and one or another of the waitresses from one of his father's restaurants, bringing a niece or younger sister who was visiting from out of town. If there were still tickets left by the time the Pescadoor party got to the arena, Knute's mother would give them to the black kids who hung around outside.

"'The more the merrier!' is what I say," Mrs. Pescadoor would say when Knute and Anne expressed embarrassment about how she ran around giving away tickets and about the strangers they were going to have to sit with—be identified with—during the show. "Don't always be such sticks in the mud all the time. . . . It's gonna be a great party!"

It was a kind of party. Mrs. Pescadoor would take the middle seat, assign the others places on either side of her. Before anyone was "allowed to sit down," they'd have to introduce themselves to everyone else in the group, and then Mrs. Pescadoor would quiz members of the group: "What's the name of the boy right to your right?" "Do you know which one's my beautiful daughter? Betchou can't remember her name!" "How about our new Negro friend—which one of you can remember *his* name?"

"Cut it out, Mom, everyone's tired of that game," Anne would say after a few minutes.

Mrs. Pescadoor would mumble something like "Excuse me"

or "I guess I better shut up." And she'd be very quiet for a minute or two. Then start up anew: "This is going to be great!" "You know, I think I love watching figure-skating more than anything else in the whole world." She'd lean across the row of people, tap, say, one of the waitresses on the knee: "Aren't you excited?" "Don't you just love figure-skating!"

"Who wants beer, who wants Coke? Hot dogs? How about some peanuts? I see the peanut man coming up the stairs. Everybody who wants peanuts raise their right hand and say, 'I want peanuts!'" "Hey, you . . . Not you, the nutty one. Good joke, eh?" "Hey, Knute, look—it's the same guy from last year, 'member? See the guy selling the ice cream? Hey, ice cream vendor—'member me from last year? Don't you remember—you sold us that carton with the bad bottom and it got all over that little girl's dress? How come they didn't fire you? No, I'm just teasing. It wasn't your fault at all, it was the manufacturer's fault. I told the girl's mother she should sue them—they owed her a new dress. But I don't think she's gotten around to it yet. Maybe though. Hey, you know . . ."

As soon as the lights came up after the show: "Now that was magnificent! Oh, I'm just so sad it's over. Aren't you sad, Stephanie? Todd? I don't know why they don't come more than once a year. But, I shouldn't be sad, right? I've just gotten to see my favorite show."

The enthusiasm would persist through the hour's drive back to their suburb, but, as Mrs. Pescadoor pulled in their drive, and she, Knute and Anne got out, walked up the steps and into the house, her mood would change. The weeks of convincing strangers they'd love the show, the hours at the arena loving them—now she was exhausted. Hanging up her coat in the front hall closet, she'd begin: "Do you think any one of those people said 'thank you'?" She particularly had it in for the waitresses. "Do you think any one of those girls even *thought* to say 'thank you'?"

"But you invited them, Mom," Anne might say.

"Of course I invited them. But that doesn't mean they were doing me a favor. If they *were* doing me a favor—if that's what they thought—they shouldn't have come."

"But why order so many tickets, Mom?" Knute might say.

"OK, forget it. Forget I ever opened my mouth. Some people say thank you, some people don't. Some people like having parties, going out with new people, having a few beers—and not worrying about who might be picking up the tab. OK, fine, forget it. Next year I'll go by myself."

"But, Mom, you don't have to go by yourself, but how about maybe just ordering tickets for Knute, me and you? Just three tickets next year, instead of twelve."

"OK, that's what you want? That's what'll make you happy? Three tickets? Next year we'll do it your way, just the three of us will go. Maybe we shouldn't go at all. It seems I'm the only one who really enjoys it."

She'd start to cry. Really cry, sob, the way a child does after holding some anger or hurt in for a long time, and then finally breaking down, letting it all push out.

Knute and Anne would help their mother sit down on one of the kitchen stools. They'd pat her back, pull her hair off her face, tuck it under her scarf again. Bring her the box of tissues from the bathroom. Agree with her that the guests hadn't been appreciative enough given that they'd had excellent seats, she hadn't charged them even a dime for them, she'd bought all the refreshments, given people rides.

*

As was mentioned back in the first chapter, every summer from before Knute could remember until he graduated from high school he and his mother had spent August with his grandparents at their lakeside cabin. His father had usually come for the last long weekend. Flying to the state capital, about an hour and a half away, where Knute and his mother would pick him up. Driving back home with them at the end.

In his twenties, remembering, Knute thought of his sister as having come with his father. His brother and sister-in-law and their kid, then kids? They did used to come out, he remembered. Usually at the end, too, it seemed. His brother generally stuck close to his father. He seemed to have formed the opinion that he and his father were somehow apart, superior. The rest of them were people who had happened to live at the same boardinghouse as he had when he was growing up. And, though they—Knute, his mother and sister—may have meant well, what purpose did their meaning well serve? Since they lacked the smarts and mental toughness necessary for getting things done. Making money. Getting large numbers of people to come to a restaurant every night, buy alcohol, eat quickly, and be satisfied.

Lying in his Pacific bed, Knute couldn't remember his

brother, or his sister-in-law, ever going in the lake, swimming. He saw them in bathing suits, on the shore. Watching over their children. Patting them. Quietly saying things like "Don't stay in the water too long, dear" or "Just ignore her, dear, if she isn't being nice to you." It seemed to him that his brother and sister-in-law had developed a way of watching out for their kids, talking to them, touching them, helping them change their clothes—without ever once looking at them. Perhaps this was a technique Susan (his sister-in-law) had learned at one of the classes it seemed she was always talking about. A more modern, more efficacious approach to child-rearing. Preventing the attachment of the reproducer from interfering with the development of the reproduced.

By and large, his brother and his family didn't figure in Knute's memories of those Augusts. Even his sister and his father rarely appeared. His grandfather had died when he was . . . Figuring it out, he must have been ten or eleven. He remembered his mother coming to the door of Miss Osterhaut's class, waving for him, calling to him in a stage whisper.

The memorial service. Afterwards groups of carefully dressed old people chatting on the sidewalk in the sun. The old lady with the hair net coming up and introducing herself as his relative, talking about the Welsh prince. Standing next to his father who kept rocking back and forth on the balls of his feet, jiggling the change in his pockets. Nodding to all the relatives.

Memory preserved Grandpa A. Rowing mornings while a younger Knute had lain in bed. Coming in the door complaining about himself to Knute's mother and grandmother. "You know, I don't think there's a fish in that lake as dumb as I am." "Jeez, I'm stiff in the morning." "Seventy-five years old, and I get winded just pulling up the darn boat."

Summers at the cabin, the adult Knute would think and smile and stretch his legs under his covers. He had so many nice memories. Going to the supermarket, his mother and him. Buying chocolate and flour for all those cakes it seemed like she was always baking. Or just standing on the tennis court they went to. Hitting balls back and forth. And scurrying around picking up balls. And just standing there feeling the sun on his face.

Sitting on the bank of the river. His grandfather fishing very seriously. Not needing to catch any trout; needing his flies to touch the surface where and as he intended them to. Studying the currents. Suddenly taking off down the bank, headed for the place where—he had now decided—he should have been fishing all along.

Knute's mother had the reputation of being able to catch trout almost at will. Other people who had summer homes near theirs joked that his mother used psychic powers or homing devices. Perhaps as a result of her easy success, she didn't take the sport very seriously. Many afternoons while Knute's grandfather worked his way among the thickets along the bank, cursing at himself, she'd lie in the sun, above the bank with Knute. Or they'd have stone-throwing contests; aiming for tree trunks—or one would toss a stone up and they'd both try to hit it with a second stone. They'd take the knife out of his grandfather's tool box and throw it. Carve their initials in the trees. Their address and phone number back home.

Knute remembered this one afternoon when his mother managed to convince his grandfather that she was even more disturbed about her own casting than he was about his. She got him to stand behind her and hold her wrists to try and help her get the feel of it. But she kept saying, no, there was something wrong, it didn't feel "natural" to her. "I don't know what it could be," her father kept saying. "It sure looks good to me. . . . Looks as good as my motion. . . . Maybe you need a better teacher than your old man."

"I don't know, Dad," his mother kept spoofing—and winking at Knute—without his grandfather ever quite catching on. "I just wish it felt natural."

Eventually Knute had signaled to his mother that if she didn't stop he was not going to be able to keep from laughing out loud.

It amused Knute how good the weather had always been in the August of his memory. When they had gone trout-fishing—whenever they had gone trout-fishing—it was a sunny late afternoon, with the sun dappling down as he lay on the bank, or sat against a tree, alternately Huckleberry Finn and a young gentleman in a French painting.

In the mornings, if they'd planned to go fishing on the lake, it could rain because that meant having to go to the back room, pick out the rubber boots and mackinaw that best fit him. A leather cap or just an old canvas rain hat. Row out on the lake amid all the muted colors, the sound of raindrops hitting the surface. Grandma always right there in the doorway with towels to dry him off the moment he returned. Helping him out of his damp jeans. Sitting him down by a blazing fire, bringing a mug of hot chocolate with little marshmallows in it. A little plate with a toasted English muffin on it.

Sometimes Knute was convinced his childhood had been completely different from his memory of it. He wasn't sure why he felt this way. There was just something insecure about memories—maybe they came from the movies, or books—or they had more to do with creativity than research.

The gypsies say you should always keep moving because places are always nicest after you've left them.

His mother and her picture puzzles. Standing by while his grandfather split firewood. Helping him stack it, make a fire. Just being by himself, watching the fire, feeling spread on his lap those biographies his mother used to keep buying him— Eleanor Roosevelt, Wilbur and Orville Wright, Thomas Alva Edison, Pierre and Marie Curie.

His room. It made him feel a little warmer, just remembering that it had existed. On one of the corners of his grandparents' house. The lake-woods corner, it could have been called, because out the window on one side, near the head of his bed, was the lake. And if he flipped around and looked out the window that was usually above his feet he could see the tree trunks, evergreen boughs, pine needles covering the ground.

His grandmother had always kept that room for him. She

had realized how much he loved it, Knute felt. And he remembered her telling him that she always saved it for him because he and his mother were her most faithful visitors. They came every summer and stayed the longest. Mornings he used to halfway move out of bed, support himself on his elbows on the window ledge, look out on the lake. The fishermen sitting in rowboats out there. Or just the sparkling of sunlight on the surface. Maybe his mother swimming through it or his grandfather rowing his heavy, green boat.

He had passed a lot of the hours of his life lying in bed. Staring at ceilings. The way roof boards go under beams. Knots. Gaps between beams. Cracks where sap had built up.

His grandmother and mother moving downstairs. The slight ringing of dishes knocking dishes. Silverware. Conversation. "I think it must be about time for me to get that lug-a-bed son of mine out of the sack," he had heard his mother say. And he had known well the next step—his mother coming up and tickling him till he couldn't do anything but get out of bed. But usually, it seemed, he had just kept lying there anyway.

When Knute was in the second grade he inherited from his sister a clock-radio that had a timer with which he could set the radio to turn off automatically. For a few years, until during their big fight his mother pitched the radio, he was in the habit of going to sleep with the radio tuned to the big pop music station. The volume turned down very low. The bass thumping. The singers talking about the burning love they had for their babies; the joy their lovers gave them; the sorrow love could bring.

Knute and his mother installed a shelf on the wall just above his bed. He would get the radio all tuned, the volume set, taking into account how much louder sounds were when it was dark. Then he'd turn out the light and get into bed. Lie on his back. Some of the singers had been mistreated, some scorned, some wanted to kiss and make up. Hearts were broken, people needed one another. And somewhere in the middle of it all Knute would fall asleep.

Chapter 6

Melanie. Melanie, Melanie, Melanie. She seemed to have established herself as the lead actress in his memories of summers at the lake. Melanie. He could be trying to recall his early childhood—he had been a normal kid, he knew, and he assumed therefore that he had spent a lot of days digging in the sand, riding a tricycle—Melanie. She had nothing to do with his *early* childhood. Melanie, first her name would come to him, then a twinge, a thirteen-year-old female body flung across his mind. Isabel arriving at the airport. Isabel and Melanie.

After the death of Grandpa A his father had bought the lakefront property from Grandma A. Not because he wanted or had any use for a vacation home. But it was an available and economical way of providing for Grandma A's old age, and Knute's mother had wanted to keep the property in the family.

Knute remembers as a teenager driving around recklessly in

an old green truck. Beer bottles on the floor. Local kids he hardly knew in the back. And lying in bed mornings imagining that that day Melanie was going to call. She was just calling to say she was getting on a plane that afternoon in San Francisco. She'd be at the airport outside the capital by ten. Could he pick her up? She had bought a one-way ticket. She didn't know how long she was going to stay. Until the morning when she saw in his eyes that he was tired of her.

When he was in college Knute wrote Melanie a letter suggesting a visit, but she never wrote back, or called.

Later he heard from his mother that Melanie was studying fashion design at a West Coast university, and when he moved out west he thought of subscribing to her alumni magazine or visiting the campus. He never did. He called information to try and get a phone number for Isabel, Melanie's mother, but there was no listing.

Melanie was one of his cousins; Isabel his mother's youngest sister. The "bad apple"—at least that's how his mother had once labeled her. Aunt Isabel: She had "deserted her family" and had "refused to recognize the responsibilities she had to people who loved her"—"to the people who had brought her into the world, and had nursed her—changed her damn diapers—and had at least tried to give her a good home and a good education."

Principally, Isabel had moved out west—when she was quite young, Knute had gathered from his mother and other family members, and from the few things Melanie had said to him.

Isabel had not waited to graduate from high school. She had said something about not needing any diploma, she'd find work in Los Angeles, modeling or acting.

Knute didn't get the impression she had ever done much acting. She had worked as a secretary at a small company. Then, according to his mother, been a "kept woman." Kept by the head, the founder of this company. A wealthy man. Apparently he had invented or figured out how to manufacture two little parts that were valuable to the Navy's jets and submarines. Something on the gyroscope line, Knute seemed to remember Melanie telling him. Eventually the man divorced his wife to marry Isabel, or her younger, firmer body, her youthful awe of his money, his invention, his admiral friends.

Or her *feigned* youthful awe. Because, in Knute's mother's story, "knowing Isabel, it was a ruse from Day One." The next step was producing Melanie. Putting in a few years for appearances. Then hoking up, or intentionally provoking [depending on his mother's mood] some physical abuse from her dear, generous husband. Melanie's version was that one night her parents were having a fight because her father was trying to persuade her mother to come back to the city with him to spend the week. But her mother always wanted to stay at their house in the country. Her father "just got carried away," Melanie said, and grabbed her mother around the neck and shook her. Then a few weeks later, after a similar argument, he set their pick-up truck rolling over a cliff into the ocean.

The day after that, Isabel, armed with film of the wreck and of lesions on her neck, filed for divorce. She had used her savings to hire a savvy divorce lawyer; they had been waiting for her husband to do something reprehensible. Isabel won custody of Melanie, the vacation property, and almost enough alimony and child support to allow the two of them to live modestly.

And, Knute's mother complained, in all the years since she'd left, Isabel had only come home to visit three times! She herself had brought her kids to their grandparents two or three times a year. Every summer she'd spent one month at home. And she had often invited her parents to come visit her. It wasn't necessarily something she wanted to do, it was a duty, or just common courtesy. Isabel had sent her mother a "post box number for an address. . . . It seems likes she's never even had a telephone installed."

Knute didn't really care. Having heard his mother's stories, and having spent one August week at the lake with Isabel and Melanie—he had been able to develop his own fantasies.

By the time he was a senior in high school, Isabel and Melanie's country house was permanently white. Clapboard. With carved eaves, Victorian-style. It stood on top of a slight hill that itself had to be on top of the cliffs above the Pacific because from their cupola it was possible to see across acres of brown fields to the green sea. White spray where the waves broke against the rocks. The rumbling of the surf. Big birds calling and turning above the cliffs, gliding down above the rocks and out to sea.

Melanie had told him that she and her mother did some modeling for department store catalogs and for a photographer in their town. Leafing through such catalogs back in the Midwest, Knute enjoyed thinking that the models for certain of the most alluring photographs were either his aunt or his cousin. He also decided that the local photographer in their town specialized in eroticism, particularly in Degas-like images of females at their toilette, undressing before their baths, etc.

Next to their house was a small paddock where Isabel and Melanie kept their two horses which they usually rode bareback. Isabel also had an old Army jeep in which she drove through the woods to the marijuana fields, the regular harvest of which was slowly but steadily making both her and Melanie extremely rich. Afternoons could be for drinking rum in the house with the red velvet curtains drawn. Evenings could be spent at the women-only bar in the town.

Late at night the wind blew between the clapboards and rattled the windowpanes. Melanie and Isabel got in their big brass beds. The former drawing her knees up under her forest green nightgown with its white trim. The latter naked, sitting up reading a spy novel, her full breasts bared to her large, sparsely furnished room.

Ah well, fantasies. There is always an unbridgeable gap between the lives one can imagine for others, and the lives they insist on living.

Isabel and Melanie. Perhaps, Knute thought, perhaps he was making a mistake, viewing it as one of his weaker periods. As the most embarrassing week of his life. What had he done really? A routine investigation of his cousin.

Being too close to a subject inevitably causes a certain blindness. He was no more required to repress his desires than anyone else was.

In Melanie's mind, he was just a blur. She never wrote. She had him mixed up with another three or four boys who had attacked her. Or not actually attacked her. He had wanted her. He had wanted her terribly.

It was all Isabel's fault for the outfit she was wearing getting off the plane from California. Or for two parts of that outfit. The cowboy shirt with the pearl snaps. And the brassiere.

It wasn't the outfit, it was how Isabel had worn it. With a significant number of snaps unsnapped. A little—or a lot of brassiere showing. And also holding her breasts. Very nice, "full" breasts.

Knute has seen Isabel three times in his life. Twice briefly before he was old enough to remember. And then, that one week at the lake, when he was fourteen. His adult idea is that she is slight, the outline of her ribs shows through her bathing suit. Brownish colored, slightly wavy hair that she keeps pulled back in a silver clasp. Tan skin, which exposure to the sun has aged prematurely.

She has a small head, he feels. Small features. When he is keeping closer to his memories than his fantasies, Isabel's breasts are fairly small, with quite a bit of bone, chest, between them. The nipples small, pointing straight out ahead.

That week she had worn almost constantly a black one-piece bathing suit that was cut very low in back and, more vitally, was a little tight on her, so it stretched across her breasts, flattening them, making her nipples more apparent and also stimulating them so they hardened and appeared pushing against the fabric. At her crotch, the tightness revealed the contours of her external labia. And a small crop of light brown pubic hairs was exposed outside the elastic.

Whenever Isabel had swum out to the raft to sunbathe, Knute had pulled the innertube into the water and floated out to watch her. On land he had a particular tree against which he stood leaning for hours, shifting his stare up and down between Isabel's breasts and her crotch as she sat at the outdoor table. Often her feet would be up on another chair and her legs crossed, so all he could see was the top of her crotch, a few hairs—plus her nipples. But, in the course of the seven warm, sunny days, there were two approximately thirty-minute periods during which Isabel sat sipping coffee, looking right past his tree out at the lake, the soles of her feet up on the seat of her chair, the way a monkey sits—the whole swatch exposed to him.

He had been happy, he liked to tell himself. For the almost fifteen years leading up to that week with Isabel and Melanie he had been happy, content. He couldn't really say that in forcing him to recognize the bull-headedness of his sexual desires—in fixating his visual curiosity for eternity on the breasts and crotches of the opposite sex . . . He couldn't really say they'd done him any favors.

The first day he and his mother had picked Isabel and Melanie up at the airport and had driven them back to the cabin. On the table outside Grandma A had served coffee, juice and her apple-spice cake. Isabel had had her coffee, talked a little. Then she had announced—as if she had a very busy life and couldn't dawdle even on her vacations—it was time for her and Melanie to take their first swim. They'd gotten up to go inside and change. Knute had asked his grandmother if there was any raking that needed doing around the swimming area. Asked *loudly*. So Isabel, walking away, toward the house, would be sure to hear. And so then, then she would think, when she came to the swimming area, that he just happened to be there too. He must be a nice boy, to be helping his grandmother with the chores. It would only be natural for him to look up as her breasts walked by.

But of course it had so happened that Isabel and Melanie arrived at the swimming area only a few moments after he and his grandmother. As Isabel and Melanie set their towels down on the bench and stepped in the water, he had to be walking along looking at the bushes with his grandmother—getting his instructions. He glanced a few times back over his shoulder, but he saw none of things he had planned on seeing.

Effectively, the whole thing, the whole week was ridiculous. He had been too young. It had been his first time. (If you didn't count taking a book and going and sitting in the hall when his sister was taking a shower. Pretending to be reading, glancing up at the door. Hoping Anne would come out without her bathrobe on. A couple times crawling to the keyhole and trying to see something when she was drying herself off.)

What could he say? Think? He had no good excuses. Sex. Females. They had been his downfall. No, they hadn't been his downfall, they'd been his salvation. Or never mind salvation—as an adult he came to the conclusion that women always had and always would direct his life. He told Martha that the only reason he worked so hard to make his diner succeed . . . Well, partly it was fear, fear that he was incapable of supporting himself. And partly he didn't want their daughters ever to even think about money.

*

Knute has found it strange, remembering how the first five days he'd hardly noticed Melanie. She'd been Isabel's side-kick. A thin, almost breastless, and breathless, form, like a shadow on one side or the other and just behind Isabel. A shadow in a light blue bathing suit with white and yellow stars.

One morning his mother had suggested he take Melanie for a hike up to the deserted hunting cabin on the hill that over-looked the lake. His mother had seemed to feel that, since he and Melanie were cousins and about the same age, they should become pals, despite the apparent lack of interest on either part—in even saying more than one forced hello and one see you later per meal.

So it was kind of a stiff morning, walking up to the cabin

and showing it to her. But, dutiful son that he was, he gave the complete tour. Showed her the trail up there that his mother and he had marked. The curtains his mother had sewn for the windows. The old broom and dust pan they'd brought up there. The secret ladder, the view from the roof.

Had Melanie been completely disinterested in him, and in the silly cabin he and his mother had fixed up? It could have been sexual tensions, anticipation. Or perhaps it was just him—his gawky body and lack of things to say—not only to attractive females—but to humans of all types who he didn't know well and who he wasn't with in some calm situation. Besides—he had been no more interested himself in taking this stiff drip of a cousin up to his mother's cabin. When he could have been down by the house standing against his tree, staring at his aunt, in her chair at the table. With her feet on the other chair, her nipples, crotch, pubic hairs.

A wasted morning at the cabin. Melanie had thanked him very politely at the end. Told her mother that it was a very nice cabin that Knute and his mother had fixed up. And—between the lines—don't ever let Knute's mother send me off alone with him again. I don't want to die of boredom and ugliness.

What had Melanie really thought about him? That had certainly been a major question of his teenage years. And, more casually, it had followed him through his twenties as well.

Perhaps nothing. Often, considering Melanie, the only conclusion he could come to was that there was nothing inside her head.

Isabel and Melanie had come on a Sunday morning, left on the next Sunday. On the Friday night his mother had taken his aunt out to dinner. He and Melanie had been left with the grandparents.

After dinner Melanie had been sitting calmly on the sofa by the radio, listening to music and flipping through old *Vogue*s. He sat in the rocker near the fire with a book on his lap, and then he went over to the stairs and went up and down them, and then went into the kitchen and held the sifter for his grandmother, and then went and sat back in the rocker again, and went up and down the stairs again. He hadn't been able to sit still or do anything for very long because he was trying to figure something out. The two nights before when Isabel had gone down to the bathroom from her room, he'd managed to time it fairly well, so he'd been stepping out of his room, and he'd glimpsed flesh before Isabel had pulled her bathrobe closed around her.

He was trying to figure out if there would be any advantage in hiding downstairs, then coming up when he heard Isabel starting for the bathroom—or maybe when she was coming back from the bathroom. She wouldn't be expecting him, and he might have an excellent view up from underneath.

Then his grandmother had suggested to Melanie that she play a game with him or work on a puzzle. "He looks like he's in need of something to do," he has remembered her saying.

Without saying a word, Melanie had gotten up, slipped the magazines back onto the shelf with the other old *Vogue*s, and come over to him where he had been standing by the fire, rocking one of the logs with the poker. "What are we going to play?" she had asked in her weary, dutiful tone.

They had played casino, which was a game Knute had never played before. Melanie explained the rules and some strategy, and they played it for about an hour, sitting at one corner of the dining room table. Slowly feeling more comfortable with one another.

Perhaps, the adult Knute has thought with amusement—perhaps he'd impressed her. A fourteen-year-old boy able to learn the complex game of casino in less than an hour. Or perhaps—no, obviously—the key had been losing. It didn't matter that *he had learned*. The key was that *she had taught him*, and—most happily—that she had then, in winning, proved herself superior.

Next he had taught her his mother's double solitaire game. It had more in common with Ping-Pong than cards—it was a question of how fast your fingers could move cards from one pile to the next.

Even at thirty Knute could almost feel Melanie's long blond hair swinging into his face as it almost had when she had jumped up, trying to get her cards onto the center pile. Then her deciding she should put her hair in a ponytail and running up to her room for one of her elastic bands. Coming back. Deftly gathering her hair up with one hand, stroking it, shaking her head, getting it all organized and then slipping the band on.

They had started to have too much fun together. His grand-mother had come over and warned them to be careful about the surface of the table, and not to jump up and down in the chairs because they were old and were precious to her. And next she had said she and Grandpa were going to bed. Which meant it was time for Melanie and him to go to bed too.

A dozen years later, lying alone in his bed, looking up at the ceiling, he tried to inhale again the warm sweet smell of Mel-anie's skin, the imitation herbal smell of her shampoo. He saw her leaning across the dining table toward him and whispering that they were going to continue playing upstairs. Slipping the cards under her sweatshirt and tucking them somewhere there. Then she had gone and kissed both their grandparents good-night, waved to him with a smile, and headed up the stairs.

She had been waiting for him in the hall when he came up. All the lights had been off. And she had been standing up very straight, against the wall. She had put a finger across her lips. To make sure he was quiet.

He'd whispered to her to follow him. Down to his room. It was the best place because it was the furthest from the stairs, furthest from their grandparents' room.

Inside his room he'd shut the door. Suggested they play on the bed, take off their shoes. They'd both crouched down, bent over to untie and pull off their shoes. He'd gotten on his bed and sat down at the head, his back against the wall. She'd sat on the end, with the moonlight coming from the lakeside win-dow and running down her left side, all white.

It had taken them awhile to hit on the next game they wanted to play. They had leaned together over the center of the bed, whispered. Double solitaire was too noisy, they had agreed. They had tried gin, but after a couple hands Melanie had whispered that gin was boring and she had never liked it. He—as always anxious to agree with opinions stated by females—had told Melanie him neither, he'd never liked gin, it was boring.

But what to play then? War, he had suggested but they had both quickly agreed it was a stupid game. Poker, that was just about the only other game they knew, except blackjack, which, they both agreed, really wasn't fun unless you had a lot of people and chips.

Melanie had suggested strip poker. If it had been left up to him . . . He'd be a celibate bachelor living in a one-room apartment across the street from a bus station, hoping only that women didn't notice when he dribbled food on his shirt and then tried to soak the stain out with cold water the way his mother had taught him.

Melanie had said she'd played strip poker before.
He'd said he hadn't.
She'd said she played it all the time with her girlfriends.
With boys though? he'd asked her.
She'd said, yes, once, with her two step-brothers.
How far had they gone? (How far had she gone!)
They'd gone all the way to underpants and then she'd lost

and so she'd had to pull up her undershirt and show them her breasts. Shrug. No big deal.

Socks had come off—his or hers—the acid and gas had fired down into his intestines. Shirts, pants.

He'd "never played strip poker before?" Without saying much more than those words Melanie had been able to give him a hard time about his naivete. The boys she knew in California had all played. Maybe, she had suggested, it was because his mother was around so much. Or maybe, he had pointed out, it was because he didn't have any step-sisters and his real sister was so much older than him.

In his twenties he realized it hadn't been all fun and games there on his bed. There had been a certain competitiveness. A being, or trying to be, older than the other. Less surprised—or "overwhelmed" was a better word. Less sexually excited is what it boiled down to.

That was sad. Fourteen and thirteen years old, they'd finally gotten to (or returned to) a point where they could enjoy at least some of their capacity for sexual pleasure, but before doing so they felt like they had to put up these fronts, pretending they already knew it all, had done it all. And also—what really annoyed him was that they had to pretend it didn't really excite them, sexual pleasure, they could take it or leave it.

He had made a bit of a fuss, he guessed. Made a fool of himself. Getting tense, snatching up his cards. She'd made a comment about how serious he'd gotten. It was only a game. Easy for her to say—still half-dressed!

He remembered her asking him, before he'd finally lost and had to take off his underpants, Was he sure he wanted to "go all the way"? Because he looked so worried, his teeth were clenched.

That's what she thought—clenched teeth were a sign of tension?

No. He had been tense. He had never quite been able to forget that he had tried to take off his underpants while still sitting cross-legged. She'd told him he had to stand up and let her see, those were the rules. Plus, she had said he had to either stand in the moonlight or turn on the light.

The funny thing was that he didn't think she had been at all interested in looking at his naked body, his penis. Certainly it could not have been impressive—he had only been fourteen. But still, he couldn't remember her doing more than glancing over at him. Like some kind of bored inspector. At the same job for twenty-five years. Just a quick glance to make sure the trunk that was supposedly full of candlesticks actually existed.

Which hadn't stopped him from fussing. Well, he did have one excuse—it was his first time. If he had known in advance that the girl didn't really look . . . Maybe he would have stood right up on the bed next to where she was sitting—so that when he took his underpants off his penis would have been in Melanie's face.

Instead, he'd made a fuss. No he wasn't going to stand up to take off his underpants. No lights. She was making up new rules at the end of the game, which wasn't fair. Would she have told him about those rules if she had lost?

"Of course," she had said. It just wasn't that big a deal, a boy seeing her naked. They hardly had anything to see anyway, they were still too young. And, she had offered, if he (was such a chicken and a prude, was her implication) . . . Nonetheless, if he wanted to stay seated and out of the light, that was fine with her. What did she care?

He had eventually agreed to play by the rules. Climbed off the bed and stood in the light. Slipped off his underpants.

He had wanted to know what they did next—start again? She had explained that they could keep going, but they didn't have to. It was optional. She didn't want him to think she was making up new rules. But if they went on and *she* lost, of course she still had clothes to take off. But if he lost, she could make him do things.

Like what kinds of things? he'd asked.

She'd said she didn't know exactly. She'd only done this with her girlfriends. Maybe they'd have to spread their legs and moan a little or take poses. Call a boy they knew up. Not identify themselves of course. But say some line like, "I'm naked for you." Then hang up of course.

She said she didn't know if Knute wanted to do this, to go

on. As far as she was concerned she was sleepy, she could just go back to her room, get into bed and go to sleep. But, going on, that would give him a chance to see her. Or, if he wanted, it wasn't normally part of the game, but she'd just take the rest of her clothes off. They didn't have to keep playing.

He'd rejected that. Unsportsmanlike. Let the game continue. As long as she agreed not to make him do anything too . . . Too . . . ? Too bad.

They had kept playing. And, by the time he'd gotten to college Knute was sure that she had tried to lose the last hands. Melanie *had* just wanted to go to bed. But, nevertheless, she'd won two games before she'd lost again. She'd had trouble thinking of anything for him to do. He'd gotten impatient, cold, cross. Finally, the first time, she'd said he could walk to the end of the hall and back, naked. The second time she had said she couldn't think of anything and wanted to just pass but he had said that wasn't right. She'd told him to walk down the stairs and back.

After she lost her undershirt he had asked her if she would stand in the moonlight so he could see. She had agreed to and it had been very nice. It was as if that had restored the gentle, companions feeling—or whispering co-conspirators feeling— they'd had before. Sneaking the cards up to his room, meeting in the hall.

He'd stretched out naked on his bed. Watched the moonlight falling over her, catching various parts, angles of her body, as she slowly turned. Holding her arms up, hands in her hair. So her small, beginning breasts were fully exposed to him.

She *had to* have enjoyed this too, he'd decided as an adult. Many days, lying on his bed by the Pacific, he had felt the two of them slipping into a trance. Without saying anything she pushed her underwear down, stepped out of it, set it aside. She came back into the moonlight and stood up straight before the window so he could see her in profile. The mullions made their pattern on the bare white skin of her face and chest. She put her left foot up on the ledge so he could see the inside of her thigh.

When she stopped modeling he'd asked her if she would do it again, this time with the lights on. The request had spoiled the mood. She'd gotten brusque again. Said she had to go to bed. He'd whimpered—they weren't going to keep playing? He'd wanted to get to the point where she had to do something for him. She'd said she was too tired. Maybe tomorrow night. Tomorrow night our moms will be here he'd said. So she'd agreed—but only under one condition—no more poker playing. He could just tell her to do something and she'd do it. One thing, then she was going to go to bed.

Of course he hadn't been able to think of anything. Given the opportunity to tell a naked female to do something, anything—he'd drawn a blank. There had been nothing but air in his brain, and too much of that besides.

Melanie had gotten pissed at him. Taken matters into her own hands. Offered to spread her legs. In a tone that suggested it was spread legs or zippo. But spread legs had seemed more than more than enough! He'd done a lot of nodding, yes, spread legs is fine.

So she'd "spread her legs" for him. She'd told him to get off the bed so she could lie down. Turn on the light. Then she'd put her hands under her thighs. Pulled them up toward her chest and apart.

Chapter 7

His first vulva!

Knute's first year in college he submitted to his English class a poem he had written about visiting a prostitute. Not having ever visited a prostitute. Inspired to a large extent by his memories of that night with Melanie.

In the poem he used the word "vagina" when in fact the male character did not have any form of intercourse with the prostitute but rather stood and admired the external features of her genitals. After Knute read the poem to his class, one of the other male students argued that Knute's diction was flawed in one important way: In this case the proper word was "vulva," not "vagina."

In his late twenties, Knute came to accept that he had not retained any memory of Melanie's vulva. That when he closed his eyes he saw a substitute image, constructed from his fantasies, memories of later girls, girlie pictures.

White, hairless. With that swollen, tumescent quality of the female pubic region.

Melanie's hair—her head hair—spread on one of the wide, dark green bands of his blanket, beneath and around her face. Her eyes open, looking directly up at his ceiling. No sense of tension in her body. She might have been made of papier-mâché. Her fingers under her knee joints. No anus, he realized. They had been at the wrong ages to see or have anuses during sexual situations.

It had seemed to go on and on. Melanie holding that pose, and still holding that pose, her lower back curved up off the bed. Him thinking, this is silly, she can put her legs down now, go to her room. One glance is plenty. There's not all that much to see. Like in an art museum. He always felt that to qualify as one who admired and appreciated art—as he did—that he should stand at least a few minutes before every painting, longer before the famous ones. And he would stand there. And he'd assume that as he stood there his sense of the painting was deepening, he was seeing progressively more and more of it. Yet whenever he tried to verbalize what he saw, it was always the same figures or shapes, landscapes; the light was always coming through the same window. He'd step up to check on how the paint had been applied. Note the cracks. Step back. It would still be the same figures and light.

Finally he had thanked Melanie, told her she must be getting cold. If she wanted to go to bed she should go to bed.

She'd put her legs down. Sat up. Still completely naked.

She'd asked him to hand her her clothes. He'd had to gather them up, hold them, bring them over to her.

This had been the nicest and the most stimulating sequence of the whole evening. Going to the corner chair to get her underpants. Then to the other chair where she'd piled the rest of her clothes. Being himself still naked, crossing the light coming in the window so that she would have been able to watch him if she had wanted.

He'd brought the clothes over to the bed and set them down in a pile next to Melanie's naked right buttock and thigh. His face passed along the white panel of her chest and abdomen, dipping into the space above her thighs.

She'd picked her underpants out of the pile. Pulled her knees up to get the underpants over her feet. Gotten up just at the last moment to get them over her buttocks, covering herself.

Next her undershirt. Pulling it out of the pile. Finding the front and back. Getting her arms through. Then pulling it down over her breasts.

Pants had gone on, covering her underwear. Sweatshirt. Zipped up. It was sad remembering.

She had taken her shoes and socks in her hand. Given him a kind of plastic smile. "Bye, Knute," she'd said. Opened his door, and then closed it behind her.

*

And then. He had often had a problem with the "and then." Or, actually, he saw himself facing two problems: First and foremost, Melanie had not decided to stay in that room with

187

him for the rest of his life, letting him lie around and walk around naked while she—sometimes with his help, sometimes by herself—dressed and undressed for him. Perhaps after a couple years they would have started lying on his bed together, getting under the covers. Pressing their bodies together. Learning to kiss. Second—the second problem—the "and then," later that night.

He'd just been a kid. He'd done what people do when they're young, and when they're old they are embarrassed to have done these things. Or perhaps good people are those who forget ever having done such things. Or maybe good people were like him, they couldn't shake their embarrassment, their memories, and for that, not for their actions, they were called good. For feeling guilty. He sure didn't know.

Time had passed. After Melanie had left his room. He'd gone to the bathroom—down the hall past her closed door. He'd spent a lot of time in the bathroom. Looking at himself in the mirrors. Watching himself piss, sit on the toilet. Studying his penis from various angles, tucked between his legs . . .

A form of meditation. In the course of which his thoughts had indeed attenuated, dissipated. Until he had entered a state in which he no longer recognized himself, nor felt in his feet the cold of the floor. Moving slightly, adjusting the position of the organ. Back, forth, under, over, in between, around. Time passing. Until the sound of his mother's car in the drive had woken him. He'd switched off the bathroom light and run back down the hall to his room. Closed the door. Jumped into bed. Under the covers.

He'd lain there a long time; it might have been as much as a couple hours. While Isabel and his mother said goodnight. Then Isabel had come upstairs. Gone back and forth from her bedroom—next to his—and the bathroom. Gotten into bed. Read for a while it had seemed from the sound. His mother had had her last glass of wine. Flipped through a magazine or two. Then she'd come up. Opened Isabel's door and said a few more words to her. Done her bathroom stuff. Finally gone to her room, and stayed there.

Had he been lying in bed waiting for his mother and aunt to go to sleep, so he could go to work? He didn't really think so. In his version he had been too excited, too riled up to sleep. Then, late at night—his defenses down—or his ability to think clearly and sensibly exhausted—he'd decided to pay Melanie a visit. To look at her again. In a bed. In her bed. Perhaps sleeping. Perhaps awake. Perhaps awake, too riled up to sleep, thinking of him. Thinking of paying him a visit but just barely lacking the boldness to do so. (Perhaps because she was the female. It was the males who were supposed to be bold.)

When he had heard no people noises in the house for some minutes he got out of bed and tiptoed down to Melanie's door. Still naked. Half of the excitement had been being naked throughout this whole time.

He had opened Melanie's door, stealthily, slowly. Looked in—like a robber or detective on television. All seemed quiet. He'd stepped in. Melanie had been asleep. The first time he had come in the room she had been on her stomach; the pillow on the floor near the head of the bed, like she'd pushed it there; her head on the mattress, her right cheek. Some hairs that had gotten out of her ponytail over her left cheek.

He'd gone over, sat on his knees on the side her head wasn't facing. Heard her slow, even breathing. Enjoyed the warm smell of her sleeping body. A slightly thicker smell than she had moving around during the day. He'd studied the little hairs on the back of her neck before the sheet. Slowly, lightly stroked her right arm where it came out from under the covers.

He'd gotten up and slowly—very slowly and carefully— lifted the covers from the right front corner of the bed and carried them back, exposing Melanie's nightgown-covered back and right side.

He'd looked at her only briefly. The forest green of her nightgown, with its white, lacy trim. He'd quickly covered her again, hurried out the door and back down the hall to his own room.

He'd stood in the middle of his room awhile. Then gone back. Stealthily opening the door again. Going back again to his place to the right of Melanie. Sat down, his legs out straight under her bed. Listened again to her breathing. Felt her warmth; a length of warmth set in the middle of the darkness and drafts of the rest of the room.

He'd studied her hair. Felt happy. Like a guard, assigned to guard a very special person the night before a big event. Make sure nothing happens to her. That she gets a good night's sleep.

He'd done his best for a while. Maybe it had also been his

job to get her up and dressed for the big event. Or maybe, he had thought at the time, if she knew I was right here, naked, watching her . . . maybe she'd be happy if I could see more of her.

He had gotten onto his knees and again slowly lifted the covers off her shoulders and worked them back, over, off her body. All the little folds, waves of her nightgown, the small of her back, the slight rise of her buttocks, folds of nightgown filling in between her thighs, finally, just above the backs of her knees, bare skin.

But then the drafts on her bare skin, or his dropping the covers a little, had disturbed her. As he—frozen by panic and fascination—had held the covers over her, she had turned underneath him onto her back. Eyes still closed, she had said to the air above her lips, "Did something happen to my covers?"

He'd dropped them. Ducked under the bed and lay down flat on *his* stomach, *his* right cheek to the floor.

Above him, Melanie, still essentially asleep, had pulled the covers up over her shoulders, turned on her stomach.

It became a challenge—Could he do this thing or not? Girl, boy, man or woman lying sleeping on that bed—it didn't matter. He had to see if, without waking the sleeper, he could remove the covers and clothing and expose the primary sexual organ.

His heartbeat and breathing calmed down. Melanie returned to her slow, soft, sleeping breathing. He got up, brushed himself off.

Melanie had been on her right side, knees pulled up slightly, her left arm on top of the covers holding them against her. Trying to keep them for herself.

And doing a good job. He had tried a couple times and hadn't been able to get them down under her arm without really jerking them, which he hadn't wanted to do because he felt sure that would wake her. So he had been stopped temporarily. Which had led to a few minutes of doubt and remorse. Going back to his room. Feeling low and mean for trying to strip Melanie without her permission and while she was asleep. But then he'd gotten a new idea for how he might succeed, and he'd gone back.

This time he had carefully pulled the blankets and top sheet out from under the end of the mattress below his cousin's feet. He'd carried the ends of the blankets forward, laying them over her side. But temporarily leaving the top sheet to keep any drafts from disturbing her.

It made him laugh to remember. Knute Pescadoor, fourteen-year-old master criminal. Slapping his hands—at the time he hadn't slapped his hands, but in his memory he had that feeling. As if removing those blankets had been like climbing in a back window, switching off an alarm. And then it had just been him, the safe, his miraculous fingers, and a whole, peaceful night to work.

Perhaps his embarrassment—the next morning, lying in bed for hours, not wanting to go downstairs and see Melanie or be seen by her. . . . And for all the years thereafter. . . . Something was out of sync. Had he ever felt so alive, so aware, as he had those two nights with Melanie?

He'd carried the top sheet up and forward, exposing as he went. Bare feet, bare ankles, bare calves, then the nightgown beginning around Melanie's knees. He had held the sheet up like a tent over her lower half. Looked under, very happily. Remembered happily her posing in the moonlight while he lay on his hands in bed. Taking her underpants off just for him. Pulling her legs up, "spreading her legs." Asking him to bring her clothes to her. Gathering them up, first her underpants from the one chair.

His arms had gotten very tired, holding the sheet up and holding it up. His face had felt very warm and nice with her nice warmth coming up to it. He'd set the sheet down and kneeled on her bed by her feet. Then put his head down as close as he could to where her underpants went through, between her thighs.

She still hadn't woken and he'd been very happy there. But then he'd moved his hands up and tried to work her underwear down. Between his face and her thighs.

"Knute, what are you doing here? What's happened to all my covers? What are you doing, Knute! Knute, no! No, Knute. Knute, what time is it?"

She'd made a lot of angry movements, trying to cover herself but not realizing that the covers had been pulled up from

193

the bottom. He'd helped her a little, straightening things out, trying to tuck them in. But she kept kicking and had ended up getting her feet tied up in the covers.

Also she kept telling him he had to get out. He had kept telling her not to worry, he was going to get out, he just wanted to help her get covered. And he was sorry, he'd told her many times he was sorry.

Of course that hadn't been worth much that night. Nor the next night when he'd made another foray. Gotten her underwear off and kind of slept with her for a while, him curled up at the bottom of the bed, between her legs.

Chapter 8

A British historian, E. H. Carr, has argued that historians living in cultures that seem to be thriving see the past as a record of progress. From the Big Bang or Garden of Eden, or wherever one wishes to start, up to the present in which the historian is writing (Victorian England or the 1960s in the U.S., for examples), and on and on, better and better.

According to Carr, those of us writing during less idealistic periods take comfort in cycles. Thus Voltaire, in the introduction to *Le Siècle de Louis XIV*, writes of the glorious Greek century of Pericles, Plato, Aristotle and Alexander, preceded, surrounded and followed by barbarism. Then the Rome of Caesar, Ovid and Lucretius. Overrun by the Germanic hordes. The Dark Ages, then the Florentine Renaissance. Then that Renaissance spreading through the rude north to France for its glorious seventeenth century—Louis XIV, Molière, Pascal, Le Nôtre.

With such an outlook, living in the eighteenth century, Voltaire didn't feel so bad. He could maintain hope. The later Louises might be mean-spirited and short-sighted. One could feel threatened by the upheavals and violence soon to come. And yet still imagine later, glorious eras—Napoleon, the rail system, the Eiffel Tower, Cézanne. Proust.

It is much the same with me and Knute. Cycles. Not only as regards cultures or history, but a constant cycling of people from year to year, schoolteacher to schoolteacher, relatives, friends . . . fights, jobs, books, beaches. . . . One picking up where the last left off. And of course change can only be slight from cycle to cycle. Otherwise—if we imagined large changes taking place—we'd be back to the idea of progress *and* its flip side—decline—what we're trying to avoid with our cyclical theories.

This book is almost done. I am only going to relate one more story about Knute and his childhood. This is not to say there is only one more story to tell. Knute's life is a repository of stories, and certainly the story that follows this digression does not describe some momentous transition; it describes a little transition.

I started working with the character Knute in 1977. As was suggested in the fifth chapter, in 1977 Knute was the protagonist in a short story about a week in the life of a young man who'd recently graduated from college and come to New York City and was working at his first job—Production Assistant at a small, academic publishing house. (Which, of course, happened to be my situation at that time.) During this week (mind you it was February—winter—and I'd been living in California; I was not at all prepared for or pleased with that February)—this Knute went berserk.

He was producing a book about criminal recidivism in New York. A very academic book. Out-of-date statistics and undecipherable equations transformed into dozens of tables. The most obvious conclusions most carefully arrived at and then lost in a swamp of large words like "aggression-response" and "delegitimization."

The young man tried to sell this book, as news, to the *New York Daily News*. He also went to the dentist for a lot of root canal work (as a way of getting out of the office). He bought himself a three-piece white polyester suit at the Planned Parenthood Thrift Shop. Had a few drinks at the King Cole Lounge of the St. Regis hotel. Yelled at one boss, slept with another. (Knute and I both have come a long way since then.)

As I've said, I wrote this out as a short story, and I remember, over the next three years, occasionally going back to it, rewriting it to make it more, or less, realistic, or longer, or shorter. Occasionally sending it out to magazines; eventually slipping it into a cardboard box with the label "Old Papers, tax junk, writing, clips."

By 1980 I was in graduate school, and I was desperate to write a novel, and I kept trying different plots, characters, voices—ending up with a lot of notebooks and folders each containing tens of thousands of lovingly and artfully selected words and not much else. One day I pulled my old Knute story out of its box and decided to try to turn *it* into a novel. I wrote a chapter 1 with my original Knute at the office, cussing at the top of his lungs at one of his bosses. And then, chapters 2 and 3 turned into Knute's memories of his childhood, in particular his memories of battling with his mother.

The childhood material seemed stronger, perhaps simpler, certainly more "commercial." More appealing. The novel made its way toward being the story of a boy, Knute, up until just after he had his first meeting with the "real world"—when he went to work for the academic publishing house.

By late 1983, though, the novel had gotten bogged down. It seemed to stretch on and on from one episode I didn't feel any need to write to a next episode that looked to be more or less the same. One November day I found myself wandering across Paris, France, weighed down with worry. How was I ever going to finish a novel for which I had lost my enthusiasm? How could I expect anyone to want to read it?

Passing some fancy clothing store, I must have been, when I decided to just skip it. Just figure out what a reasonable length—and a reasonable amount of dramatic muscle—for a standard contemporary American novel is, and how much of Knute's life story I would be able to tell over that length, and cut the novel off there. By the time I reached the Luxembourg Gardens I had decided to end the novel where it now ends, after the upcoming story.

This may seem to reveal a shameful laziness. But, of course, in my view of human psychology—which may be to say in my view of my own psychology—shameful laziness walks hand in hand with frightening industry. And, such things notwithstanding, I don't want my readers to feel that I picked some arbitrary de-structure for this novel out of the thin, Parisian air.

There is a standard American novel paradigm in which at the beginning there's a protagonist with a problem, and at the end there's the same protagonist with a solution; or, more ironically, more literarily, at the end the protagonist has come to recognize the problem and, at the very end, to accept that there is no solution. That day walking across Paris—thinking about Knute and the incidents of his life, restructuring *Knute, and Knute Again*—I began to realize that up till then in my novel I had been misrepresenting my attitude toward this paradigm. I began to sense the tension which was prepared to hold my book together, the conflict between the young author's excessive obedience to and his adolescent rebellion against his form.

To return to the cyclical theory. From early childhood Knute seems to have had this Dr. Jekyll and Mr. Hyde quality. For long stretches he seems to be unusually dutiful, unusually detached; then he pounces on someone, or goes on a rampage, becomes desperate, explodes, or tries to. And then he returns to his dutiful, detached self. Throughout his life he continues cycling between these two personae. As he gets older, his thinking becomes more sophisticated, and it becomes possible for him to recognize the cyclical nature of his life. But his greater understanding does little to liberate him. And there is no one absolute, novel-ending moment when it all—or even a great deal of it—becomes clear to him. His life is swamped with thinking, with reflection; he is forever beginning to realize how it all fits together.

Chapter 9

In Knute's not significantly inaccurate version, from the middle of his ninth-grade year through his freshman year of college he didn't ice-skate. And he wouldn't have started skating freshman year except one November evening at the campus snack bar he noticed a girl with long blond hair, blue eyes, pale skin and a nice round face. She was sitting in a booth with a male student he didn't know, and as he walked by with his packet of candy, she tilted her head to look up at him and smiled.

And then the next night he saw her at a party in a friend of a friend's dorm room. The room was packed and smoky, the music very loud; but he saw her across the room and she looked directly at him and smiled, and then she shook her head, to swing her blond hair back off her cheek, and she held it back behind her ear with her hand and smiled again.

A friend told him her name was Deborah, she was a sophomore from Providence, Rhode Island, and she hung around with an "artsy-craftsy, modern dance kind of group." Knute began looking for her in the dance studio when he went swimming at the gym. He never saw her there, but once when he was walking home from his swim he saw her walking across the quad, wearing a deep red-purple leotard.

Afternoons when he was a freshman, Knute often sat at his desk by the window of his fourth-floor dorm room. Sometimes studying, watching the dusk come on, sometimes writing to his parents or friends back home, watching other students pass on the street below, monitoring the traffic patterns, the shifting alliances of campus social life. By mid-January he had become aware that a certain group went skating on the campus pond most afternoons around three-thirty or four. And one afternoon he saw Deborah skipping down the road, arm in arm with some members of this group.

About fifteen minutes later he put on his jacket and went out, headed in the direction of the pond. He didn't follow the road around and down the hill, though; he took a path between some classroom buildings, ending up on the hill overlooking the pond. Arms crossed on his chest he stood watching the skaters darting about, skating arm in arm, yelling to one another, moaning and laughing when they fell. He watched Deborah, a strong skater, her hands clasped behind her back, by herself circling around and around the rim. Broad and soft in the hips. Pulled over her ears a brown knit cap with a fuzzy ball on the top. Her long ponytail lying against the back of her ski sweater.

That night after dinner he went to the pay phone in the lobby of his dorm and called his mother and asked her to send his skates. The afternoon they arrived he headed to the pond and skated until Deborah's group showed up. That afternoon, though, Deborah wasn't part of it. Nor did she come the second afternoon. But on the third, Knute watched her walk up, skates hanging over her shoulder. She jostled her friends for a position on the bench so she could put on her skates.

As she began skating around the far corner of the pond, Knute glided over to her.

She said hello and that she had been wondering when they were going to meet.

He said his name was Knute and began skating right next to her.

She said her name was Deborah.

Knute's attraction to Deborah was inspired by her soft body and ready smile, the comfort and encouragement she seemed both able and willing to supply. He was sure he would be happier if—instead of going to bed every night in his drafty room, listening to his roommate trying to tune in enemy fishing boats on his ham radio—if around eleven, say, he could walk over to Deborah's, maybe she'd fix him tea, or a Scotch on the rocks, they'd review their days for one another, opinions, pet peeves. Undress and hang up their clothes, stretch out. . . .

If he had explained this to Deborah she might have found it a little prescribed or presumptuous. But Knute didn't explain his interest to Deborah; he said nothing. Just skated around the pond at her inside elbow.

A few times she glanced over at him and smiled and tilted her head and raised her eyebrows slightly to signal that she was ready for him to start up a conversation.

After a few laps he said, "I like your hat." This wasn't true. There was something about that hat. . . . He wasn't sure what it was. But he didn't like that hat. He liked Deborah's long blond hair and how clean she kept it and how clean it smelled. He liked the round cheeks of her face and rear.

"Thanks," she said concerning the hat. "My dad brought it back from England for me."

He told her to stop, and he took her by the elbow and held tight as he swiveled and leaned against the edges of his blades to stop. He proposed going for a walk.

She looked sideways at him. "You want to stop skating already?"

He nodded.

Somewhat confused, she wrinkled her brow and agreed to go with him.

Continuing to grip her elbow he led her off the ice. They took a long walk around the back of the campus. They ate dinner together at her dorm. As they were finishing, he told her he had a bottle of pear brandy back in his room that he'd never gotten around to drinking. Maybe it would be good to have with coffee.

They went first to his room to get the brandy, then to hers where she had a percolator, grounds and candles. Some hours later Knute was sitting naked with his legs crossed on her bed which was on the floor of her dorm room. Deborah was kneeling behind him, wearing a silk bathrobe her father had brought her from Japan, and massaging Knute's back.

In the first chapter I referred to the questions that, as a college student, Knute would be asked by female companions—

203

such as Deborah. In complete contrast to Knute, her adolescent sexual desires were accompanied by an insatiable curiosity about the men to whom she was attracted and/or with whom she had intercourse. Not long after she and Knute had begun their walk, she had begun pressing him to answer question after question regarding his interests, his opinions, his past. Yes, she had asked him what the worst thing he could ever remember doing was. (And he had been on the verge of telling her about how he'd broken Toni's arm, but had opted instead for the time, in tenth grade, when he had stolen a motorcycle, ridden it into the city and crashed it in a ditch in back of his father's restaurant.)

Now, in mid-massage, she wanted to know, Why didn't he like ice-skating?

"I don't like ice-skating?" he asked.

"Well, it seemed like you only came out to meet me. Didn't you? I mean, would you have gone skating otherwise?"

Knute laughed. "No, probably not."

"But why not? You're a very good skater."

"Oh, jeez," Knute said. "Why did I give up ice-skating?"

"Well, yeah, for instance. And why did you want to go to all the trouble of having your mother send you your skates, and then you just wanted to drag me immediately right off the ice?"

"Deborah, these questions are complicated. This is only our first date, isn't it?"

*

When Knute was in the fifth grade, his mother signed him up to play on a kids' hockey team. White's Steel & Wire, it was called; White's Steel & Wire being the sponsor, the business that donated the uniforms. In the Pescadoors' suburb, there were three hockey teams for kids his age. Mrs. Pescadoor chose White's because it was the team their friend Doug played on.

The first afternoon Knute practiced with White's, Mrs. Pescadoor was standing at rinkside with her skates hanging over her shoulder, and the coach asked her if she was interested in skating with the team. Within a few weeks he was letting her help organize the drills, and then he named her assistant coach. At the games, she sat on the bench with the team, and he assigned her to coordinate when the different units went on and off the ice.

She appointed herself team statistician. When she had signed Knute up to play on White's, the coach had not been in the habit of keeping more than a casual record of which players scored and assisted on each goal. Mrs. Pescadoor proposed doing a more comprehensive, National Hockey League–level job. To each game she brought a bookkeepers' notebook and a green plastic case full of colored pencils she had sharpened at home. In the course of the game she would record not only the goals and assists, but also: how many minutes each player was on the ice; which players were on the ice for each goal White's or its opponents scored; and which players were penalized for how many minutes and for what infraction.

A few times each season she would make a chart displaying the statistics. It was a major undertaking, the chart (lacking decals of flowers, cars, trolls, and larger and more exacting in detail, but otherwise similar to the charts she had made for the nightclub manager, Nick Pescadoor). She had to have the dining table at home for at least a week. The family could try to find a corner to eat on, she'd say, or they could use the coffee table in the living room, or the Ping-Pong table down in the basement. She didn't care; she needed the large flat surface *and* the light, so she could make her tabulations, organize the data and record it as legibly as possible.

She first borrowed the big adding machine Ilena used to keep the Nick's Place books; then she had Ilena order her one of her own just like it. According to her system, pieces of typing paper had to be taped together to make one sheet large enough to include (down the lefthand side) all the players and (in columns proceeding across to the right) all the statistics. Colored lines had to be drawn precisely parallel and perpendicular. The final inscribing of the compiled statistic in its proper column and row had to be done with the utmost care, preferably without anyone else being in the dining room, let alone anyone trying to ask her a question or—"Don't even dream of it"—touching the table.

When the chart was finished Mrs. Pescadoor wouldn't allow it to be folded or rolled up. Doug had to come over to the house before practice. He and Mrs. Pescadoor would pick the chart up by the edges. Gradually beginning to move sideways—positioning their bodies so as to protect the chart from any wind—crossing one leg over the other—moving as slowly—but steadily—as possible out to the station wagon. Knute going ahead to open the doors.

At the rink the chart would be moved from the car down into the locker room using the same system—Mrs. Pescadoor and Doug on the edges and trying to keep the wind in the parking lot from covering the chart with dust or causing wrinkles, or rips; Knute on the doors. Doug calling out to all kids seen or anticipated: "Out of the way, please, the chart's coming. We've got the chart."

"The chart's coming! They've got the chart!" the kids made a chorus. And they'd get very officious, pushing one another out of the threesome's way, telling one another to "get back, the chart's coming." "Be careful, they've got the chart."

Practice would be delayed while the kids crowded around where the chart was taped to the wall. Finding out what their "stats" were. Comparing theirs with their teammates'. Asking Mrs. Pescadoor all sorts of questions: She knew even how many *seconds* they'd played? What were "plus-minus averages" [one of her statistics] really? How had she been able to make such straight lines? Was it really hard? Would she let them help next time?

Being assistant coach of White's was the nicest part of Mrs. Pescadoor's life those years. She loved the head coach, Tom Stepanovich. He always seemed happy to see her, happy to listen to her suggestions for strategy. She had great fun with the drills he invented.

There was "Condemonium," which used yellow rubber cones such as are used on highways and streets to mark temporary detours or lanes. Mr. Stepanovich worked as a fireman in the city, and he had "borrowed" from the fire department two dozen of these cones. He and Mrs. Pescadoor would scatter them on the ice, sometimes in geometric formations, sometimes more randomly.

The cones were obstacles. The team would scrimmage or kids in twos and threes would practice passing back and forth as they skated up ice, and they would have to look sharp to make sure they didn't skate or pass into any cones. Which sometimes during the drill Mr. Stepanovich and Mrs. Pescadoor would move around, et cetera.

Another drill was "Buddha the Eskimo," Mrs. Pescadoor's favorite. She or Mr. Stepanovich would sit cross-legged in front of one of the goals wearing a mask and a very puffy, red, down jacket. Her or his arms folded across her or his chest. At first the mask was an ordinary goalie's mask, then they started adding plastic Halloween masks—Frankenstein, the devil. . . .

The rules were that each player in turn had to try and softly shoot the puck on either side of the Buddha and into the net. If he missed the net, or hit the Buddha, he was eliminated from the drill and had to go wait on the side. If he shot too hard, even if the puck went into the net, he was also eliminated. The trick was to be able to shoot softly and accurately.

"The thing about Coach Stepanovich," Mrs. Pescadoor told her husband, "is that he's not ashamed to enjoy himself. Sometimes I think most people when they get to be adults . . . I don't know, they want to hide. They're too serious."

For his part, at least the first four years, Knute also enjoyed playing for White's, and for Coach Stepanovich. Then as now he liked having a schedule, knowing that he was supposed to be on his way to or from, or be at, some place, some activity. From late October through March, the hockey practices and games made up a significant portion of his schedule. Most every Tuesday and Thursday afternoon and Saturday morning, he knew he'd be skating with the team.

He also enjoyed *the power*. White's Steel & Wire was an extremely good kids' hockey team. In Knute's hometown it is still believed that, in Knute's third year, White's became the first American kids hockey team ever to win a playoff game against a Canadian team. In Knute's first four years, the team only lost three games, only one to an American team.

The reason for this success had little do with Knute, everything to do with Doug. In his genes Doug possessed the means to ice-skate a great deal faster than most humans and, while skating this rapidly, to push a hockey puck on the end of his stick, or pass, catch or shoot a puck. And, thanks in part to Mrs. Pescadoor, early in life Doug put a lot of time in on the ice developing these talents. And, further, he was much more dogged and enthusiastic than the average kid.

He became one of the best American hockey players of his generation. By the time he was fourteen sportswriters had begun using the phrase "best in the state." He was given a scholarship by a college renowned for the quality of its ice hockey. After college he was signed by a National Hockey League team, and he ended up playing two and a half weeks for this team, and two years for one of its minor league affiliates.

Doug's superiority was most manifest when he was in elementary school because so many of the other players were still learning how to skate, never mind how to skate quickly or how to handle the puck—or how to pass it back and forth, work with teammates. In hockey a team generally has five skaters and a goalie on the ice at any one time. Often Doug found himself playing against units that included only one or two kids who could move effectively on ice. If he was in the mood, he could skate after whoever had the puck; when he caught up to the kid he could take the puck off his stick and onto his own; and then Doug could skate by or around any of the opposing team who happened to find themselves between him and their goal. Most of the young goalies were a little afraid of the puck, particularly when the renowned Doug Levitt was about to shoot it at them. Often the only outstanding questions were whether Doug would try a long shot and miss, or whether the goalie, in trying to protect himself, would intervene between the puck and the goal. Otherwise White's Steel & Wire would score again.

In hockey, players are divided into units that go on and off the ice together, rotating every minute or two as they get tired. There are pairs of defensive players and the offensive "line," a threesome composed of a center, a left wing and a right wing. Doug was one of White's centers; Knute was one of its wings. Mr. Stepanovich let Doug and Knute play on the same line together, since they were good friends. As a result, Knute had quite a bit of success. He himself was not a great skater, puck-handler or shooter, but, at least in the beginning, he was better than average, and he was also taller than average with much longer arms. As was mentioned in the third chapter, this made it possible for Knute to park himself on one side of the net and watch Doug chase down the puck and bring it up ice and past the defense. And then all of a sudden Doug would whip him a pass from behind the net or across the ice and—if Knute wasn't too busy studying the puckers in the ice surface, or seeing if he could make the ice melt by leaning hard on his stick or rubbing the blade rapidly back and forth—he'd catch the pass and sweep it under the goalie's legs and into the net. "Goal Pescadoor, assist Levitt," he'd hear the announcer say over the public address system.

Knute developed an inflated sense of his own abilities. Thanks to Doug he scored and assisted on so many goals, and his line was so obviously the key to the team's phenomenal success . . . It was the obvious conclusion—Levitt and Pescadoor were an unbeatable combination, the two best hockey players in the region, the state, perhaps in the nation.

Until he came to this conclusion, Knute had not thought of himself as an athlete, and it hadn't bothered him that other people weren't impressed with his athletic abilities; that, for example, when teams were being picked in gym class he was often one of the last left waiting. It wasn't part of his identity, athlete. He saw himself more as the next great black singer. Afternoons when his mother was out doing errands, Knute would get her dark glasses out of the kitchen drawer, go down to the basement and turn the organ up to full volume, push the bench out of the way, jump up and down and grind his hips, bang out chords with both hands and sing. His "baby" had done this or that, he loved her or he didn't love her anymore—

Knute sang whatever pop lyrics came into his head, sometimes opting for a growling, guttural sound, sometimes practicing his falsetto.

Nevertheless, it appeared to him that, almost in spite of himself, he'd turned out to have some particular ability that made him a very good hockey player. Maybe it came from his mother. Or just from all the times she'd taken him skating. Who knew? But there he was—the second highest scorer on the very best team in the state.

Occasionally, after he'd had a particularly productive game, he could go on a bit to his teammates. He didn't boast so much as offer suggestions. "The thing you've gotta work on is learning how to get position. You can't be afraid to get right up there near the goalie, and you can't let the other team push you out of there. It takes toughness. But then you're ready to bang the puck in when it comes. Position, a lot of being good at this game is knowing what position to take and then—"

"Yeah right, Pescadoor," was one of his teammate's response to that particular suggestion. "Put you out there with anybody but Levitt and you wouldn't score a goal all season."

"I don't know," Knute said softly. And then he added, as if curious as to his teammates' opinions on the subject, "How many goals, and how many assists, do you think Doug would get if he wasn't playing with me?"

"You're nuts," someone said.

Knute shrugged, as if still waiting for the definitive answer.

*

Toward the end of Knute and his mother's third season with White's, Mr. Stepanovich began having an affair with the mother of one of the other boys. It came to be more than just an affair; they continue to meet for lunches and tennis, and to have lengthy talks on the phone together. Their sexual relations lasted more than ten years. A few times since the affair began the woman's husband has been offered attractive jobs in other states. The woman has told him that, while she wants to stay married to him and to continue to live with him, if he takes any out-of-state job, they will have two separate homes. She isn't leaving Tom Stepanovich.

When the affair was beginning, Mr. Stepanovich often talked to his wife about this woman and the "friendship" he was developing with her. The woman teaches women's studies and is active in local feminist groups; often Mr. Stepanovich would bring home to his wife and daughters some of the things he'd learned from her. The role of clothes in the subjugation of women; anthropological findings regarding female-dominated societies and the sexual division of labor in primitive tribes; the cult of the Virgin; campaigns to eliminate sex-role stereotyping in educational materials. Subconsciously, the first Mrs. Stepanovich knew what all this talk indicated, but she found it easier and more pleasant to leave her knowledge in her subconscious. Mr. Stepanovich felt he *should* be honest, tell his wife what he was doing, but he could never quite find the words, a way to get his wife to sit down and then for him to start explaining everything. Often he'd tell himself instead: It was bad enough that he was having an affair with another woman—having sex with her, loving her—she herself a married woman. On top of all that, was it really so nice to force his wife to listen to all the details? His wife who'd never done anything to deserve the way he treated her. Who'd given him—made with him, through the act of love-making—two beautiful, intelligent, fun daughters. She had nursed those children, cleaned up after them when they got sick or wet their beds, read stories to help them get to sleep at night. Helped them make presents and decorations at Christmas, Halloween costumes. Hand-painted Easter eggs and big Easter hunts with all the kids on the block. . . . Mr. Stepanovich felt a sharp yet satisifying pain and sense of helplessness when he would watch his wife—busy with household chores or helping the girls sew, working with them on their homework—and he'd think how almost daily he cheated on this woman and he would recall all the motherly or kind things she had done.

Mr. Stepanovich and his lover both worked in the city, and their spouses seldom had any reason to be there, so usually this was where they met. After a while they rented a one-room apartment in a black neighborhood. They both moved in almost exclusively white societies; they assumed they would not be found out there. And, during the first year and a half before they decided to tell their spouses about the affair, only one person did find them out—Mrs. Pescadoor.

About halfway through Knute's fourth season, Mrs. Pescadoor drew the obvious conclusion from the way her coach and this team mother would move off to the side and talk with one another before and after every practice. The mother resting her hand on his forearm; he occasionally touching her cheek.

At first Mrs. Pescadoor was stunned. Every time, every

practice, for weeks after she sensed what was going on. She'd tell herself she wasn't going to look this time, but it was as if she could feel them in the hallway outside the locker room, drawing closer, touching. She'd glance over, just once quickly. It was impossible and obvious.

She went through a second phase in which she yelled at the windshield of her car that the other mother was a slut, a whore, a filthy whore. With her tight black sweaters and knee-high black leather boots she'd lured Coach Stepanovich away from wife, family, team.

Then Mrs. Pescadoor decided that the fact that it was adultery was none of her business. She wasn't married to Tom Stepanovich, never would be, never wanted to be. She was the assistant coach of White's Steel & Wire and the mother of one of its players. It was bad for the team, potentially devastating to the boys, to have for a coach a man who had ceased to care about them, who had his hand in one of their mothers' underwear every night.

One afternoon after practice Mrs. Pescadoor overheard Mr. Stepanovich saying something to the mother in a confidential tone, and she heard the word, Katz's—which, she realized, meant the two of them were planning to rendezvous at Katz's Delicatessen in the city. She dropped Knute off at home and drove into the city, parked her car in a garage a few blocks from Katz's, and waited in the shadows of a doorway opposite the deli. After about an hour Mr. Stepanovich walked up; the other mother arrived a few minutes later. A few more minutes later Mrs. Pescadoor watched through the window as the couple leaned over the middle of their table and kissed, Mr. Stepanovich seeming to be pushing both of his hands under the table, onto the woman's knees, thighs. Mrs. Pescadoor stepped to the door of the delicatessen, pushed it open, and walked over to the couple's table. "The jig's up," she said. "You've had your fun and games."

The woman rolled her eyes and leaned her head on her hand. Mr. Stepanovich reached to take Mrs. Pescadoor by the hand, to try to calm her down.

She jerked her hand away. "Don't try anything with me," she said. "I'm not so easily swayed."

The woman rolled her eyes again. "Maybe you should sit down," Mr. Stepanovich said.

Mrs. Pescadoor shook her head. "Don't worry, I'm not going to tell on you. But you"—she looked at the woman—"you are going to switch your son to another hockey team immediately. And you"—she looked at Mr. Stepanovich—"will not coach White's Steel & Wire after the end of this season." The glint of a smile lit Mrs. Pescadoor's face. "That's my offer," she said.

Mr. Stepanovich and his lover were as much stunned by Mrs. Pescadoor's arrival and presentation as they were in agreement with her demands. But, as they reflected after she exited—in her own wacky way, Mrs. Pescadoor was right. Given the morals of their community and their own limited capacity for discretion, at the very least Mr. Stepanovich was going to have to quit coaching in the fairly near future. Or the affair would have to end.

The following September, writing to the parents of the kids on the team, Mr. Stepanovich announced his resignation and said he thought Mrs. Pescadoor was the perfect person to replace him. And for about a month both the players and the parents seemed happy with this, and she was indeed going to be the new coach. But, in early October, about a month before the first practice, one of the mothers, a Mrs. Clark, called all the other families. She argued that they hadn't signed their sons up for White's merely so the boys could play ice hockey. They had been trying to provide the boys with an opportunity to be with other boys. . . . "The coach serves as a father-figure . . . role model . . . " Further, "Mrs. Pescadoor cannot be going in the boys' locker room. . . . It's just going to be too problematic, her trying to watch out for the boys' safety and maintain order."

There was a parents' meeting at which it was determined that none of the fathers either had the time or wanted to coach the team. And so perhaps Mrs. Pescadoor should be given the job. But the group agreed that if Mrs. Clark could find a male in the community who loved working with kids, someone like Tom Stepanovich, that would be best.

It took Mrs. Clark a lot of calling around, but finally she came up with Mr. Robert Holmgren, a chemical engineer who had recently moved to the town from the East and who had a son who played hockey and was the right age to play on the team. Mr. Holmgren had never coached kids before, and he didn't know how to skate. But he had always wanted to be a coach, and he said he and his son were great hockey fans, they'd often gone to National Hockey League games. He felt sure he could do a good job. Especially since he'd heard the team was unbeatable; he'd heard it had a superstar, the Levitt boy.

Mr. Holmgren was given the job, and he took it most seriously. Before the first practice he studied a number of books on hockey and on coaching children. He took notes on file cards and developed lists of the fundamental hockey skills thirteen- and fourteen-year-old kids should be mastering and of the best drills for developing those skills. He drew up a chart of what he was going to do and what he wanted to accomplish in each of the practices preceding the first game.

He called Mrs. Pescadoor. He said he understood from Tom Stepanovich that she had been the assistant coach of the team and that she had played a key role in the team's success. He appreciated her having given so much of her time, and he was sure she had innumerable talents. She and Tom could hardly have been more successful. Nonetheless, he had reviewed the situation carefully and had tried to think about the dynamics— a boys hockey team, a new coach coming in, bringing with him a slightly different approach to coaching. He felt it would be best if this season she stayed on the sidelines with the other mothers. He just had the sense, maybe he was wrong, but he felt things would go more smoothly if the kids perceived just one authority, in this case him. And, speaking as one parent to another, he thought they could both agree that often parents get over-involved in their sons' athletic activities.

*

Knute didn't take it nearly as hard as his mother, but there were some things about the coaching change that struck him as wrong. Primarily they were visual impressions he had. Mr. Stepanovich had been six feet tall with fairly broad shoulders and a bushy moustache. He'd gotten out there on the ice, in his big skates, taking long strides, pushing off hard on his edges. Sometimes, having fun, he had gone into the corners with kids, tried to muscle them off the puck. Even Doug couldn't get away most of the time.

And then there was Mr. Holmgren. Holding a megaphone to his face—and still he had a thin, squeaky voice. He was shorter than a lot of the kids, shorter than his own son, several inches shorter than Knute himself. He couldn't skate, he didn't even seem to own a pair of skates. He'd just stand off to one side near center ice, right in the way of where the wings normally would have been skating. He'd try to bark out the commands: "Try to keep your heads up while you're carrying the puck, kids." "Head-man the puck." "Relax your hands when you take a pass." The mousy voice, the street shoes—it got to seem like they didn't have a coach, they were just a bunch of kids in uniforms skating around, with this little man keeping a megaphone trained on them.

Mr. Holmgren had split Knute and Doug up. Not deliberately, it was just that, instead of letting friends play with one another, Mr. Holmgren had decided to use a "more professional" system, putting the best players on the first line, the second best on the second, et cetera. During one of the practices he had staged a mock tryout, timing every boy skating backwards and forwards; grading the accuracy and power of their shots, their passing, checking, overall team play. On the basis of the results, Doug, of course, was assigned to the first line, Knute to the third.

Knute told himself he didn't really care. For one, why should he always get to play with Doug and score so many goals? Let one of the other wings have a chance. Plus, ice hockey, sports—he knew he was no athlete, and he wasn't even interested in being one. If he hadn't played with Doug the year before, he probably wouldn't have scored a single goal all season. He might have even left the team.

In outlining the tryout, Mr. Holmgren had said it was time they started getting used to what it was going to be like when they went to play for the high school team, or in college—the NHL if any of them wanted to try and go that far. Knute had no such plans. He was finding that his voice had much the same rich tone and irresistible power of a certain English pop star's, particularly when he played that star's latest hit record while he himself played his organ and sang.

The year before, Knute had started playing music with some of his friends. Afternoons after school when he didn't have hockey practice, he often went over to the basement of a friend's house where they had drums set up and an organ he could play. In his ninth-grade year—after Mr. Holmgren had taken over as coach—one day when there was a hockey practice scheduled, Knute's friends told him they wanted to have a meeting to choose a name for their band and plan how to start looking for gigs. Knute could have asked his friends to postpone the meeting until the next afternoon, but he decided it wasn't worth the hassle. He didn't see any reason why he couldn't miss one practice.

He never called his mother to try to explain this to her, though, and so when, as always, she went to the rink to watch the practice, and Knute didn't show up, she became convinced he'd been hit by a car, or kidnapped. The band's meeting was cut short by a call from Mrs. Lefferts, who first asked if Knute was there and second told him to get his stuff ready and wait at the door—Mr. Lefferts would be there right away to pick him up.

Therefore, a few Tuesday afternoons later when one of Knute's friends learned that a certain group of girls—including Karen, Knute's favorite—was headed downtown to go shopping, and Knute and his friend decided to follow them, Knute made a point of telling Doug to tell his mother he wasn't going to be able to make it to practice that day.

When he got home late that afternoon, he found his mother curled up in her bed, her eyes red from crying. Subconsciously, he knew the whole story. For starters she was upset that he'd skipped practice; and somewhere further along she was a failure as a mother or she was wasting her life. He asked her if there was something wrong.

Mrs. Pescadoor shook her head no, buried her face in the pillow and started crying again.

He stepped over to the bed, patted her gingerly on the shoulder. "Mom," he said. "What are you so upset about? Doug told you that I wasn't coming to practice, didn't he?"

She nodded, sniffled, tried to wipe her eyes on the pillow. She turned onto her back to look up at Knute. "I understand," she said. "I really do understand. It's just—" She choked, coughed. "It's just—"

"It's just what, Mom?" Knute asked, sitting down on the edge of the bed by her legs.

"Oh, Knute," she said. "I just destroy everything. I've lost all my friends. I've wrecked the Stepanovichs' marriage. I—"

"Mom," Knute patted the covers above her knee.

She sat up, reached for a tissue and wiped her eyes. "You shouldn't have to listen to all this stuff," she said.

"It's OK," he said, patting above her knee again.

She took a deep breath, shook her head. She leaned and fished a cigarette out of the pack on her bedside table. Lit it, took a deep drag. "I don't know why I let myself get into these states, Knute. I'm a sick woman."

"You're not a sick woman, Mom. Maybe you're just . . . I don't know, maybe you're just tired."

She cackled. "That must be it. I'm tired. I'm tired of sitting around on my duff day after day after day."

She took a long drag on her cigarette, set it in the ashtray and climbed out of bed. She stepped into the bathroom, washed her face, brushed her hair, retied her scarf.

When she came out of the bathroom she was shaking her head. "You wanna know who is *really* sick?" she asked.

"Who's that?" Knute asked.

"Holmgren."

Knute smiled, relieved to be off the hook. "Yeah, he was coaching his megaphone again?"

Mrs. Pescadoor laughed, nodded, smiled. "You're right, I don't know what I was doing lying up here crying. I should have been laughing. The first time in history a guy who can't skate tried to coach a hockey team."

She got another tissue, blew her nose. "Oh, I don't know. Listen to me talk, Mrs. Know-It-All. My son misses two practices and I'm up here in my bed crying my eyes out like he's just run off and gotten married or something. Right?"

"Yeah, I guess," Knute said.

She reached and ran her hand through his hair, pushing it back off his forehead. "What did you ever do to deserve me, right?"

Knute shrugged, felt tired. It was irrelevant whether he deserved her or not. She was his mother.

For the next few weeks he went faithfully to the practices and games. But then White's Steel & Wire lost not just one game, but two in a row.

When the second game ended, it looked to Knute like Mr. Holmgren was going to cry. The coach sat down on a bench in the back corner of the locker room and covered his face with his hands.

Knute went and sat down next to him. "Maybe they just had a really good day," he suggested quietly.

Mr. Holmgren shook his head. "After more than four years we finally hit a team on its good day?"

Knute shrugged. "Maybe."

"No." Mr. Holmgren continued shaking his head. "Oh god, the number of things I did wrong out there. Four years you'd never lost a regular season game. Until I come along."

Knute patted his back gingerly. "It's not your fault. We were the ones playing. I know I wasn't checking right. Jeez, I think I was on the ice for both of the last two goals they scored."

"It doesn't matter." Mr. Holmgren kept shaking his head, covering his face with his hands. "I keep trying to tell myself it's only a game—it's only two games—two games—god, Bob—two games—I—"

When he got into the car Knute told his mother he wanted to quit the team.

She reached and patted his thigh. "I know it feels bad," she said. "You've never lost two games in a row before. Imagine that! In your whole life you've never lost two games before! But it is only two games. You guys'll probably win every other game for the rest of the year, and you'll forget you ever lost these two."

Knute turned to face his mother. "*I* know the losses aren't important. But I feel like nobody else knows that. It's just getting too serious."

"Why do you say that?"

He described his conversation with Mr. Holmgren, adding at the end, "And, you know, in a different way, I think you take hockey too seriously too."

"How can you say that!"

"Oh, you know."

KNUTE, AND KNUTE AGAIN

"Oh no, I don't know. You can't accuse me of being one of these parents who's only interested in winning."

"No, I don't accuse you of that. I know you just like skating, you wish you could be out there skating with us, you wanted to be the coach and all. But getting so upset when I miss one practice—I just don't think it's right. It's too serious."

The next practice was scheduled for Saturday, and instead of going that morning Knute got up early, left his mother a note, got on his bike and headed out of town and then way out into the country to the small residential area where Karen lived. As he was riding back around past her house for the second time, he saw her and her mother bringing some packages in from the car. She saw him too, and they talked for a while in the driveway; then her mother came out and invited him to have lunch with them. Afterward he and Karen went down to the basement; she had just bought a black female singer's latest record and she was anxious to listen to it. He hadn't realized she loved the same kind of pop music as he did. She had thought he was into a different style, a kind of white pop music that she hated. She told him she had been trying to figure out interesting ways to play the songs she liked on her viola, since it was the only instrument she knew how to play. He insisted she play some for him, and after she'd played her pop repertoire, he urged her to go on, play the classical pieces she knew.

Around five Karen's mother called from the top of the stairs to ask Knute if he didn't think he should be calling his mother to at least tell her where he was.

225

Since it was getting dark, his mother said she was going to drive out to get him. To his surprise, she didn't sound at all moody on the phone. She didn't seem at all upset that he'd missed another practice.

He sensed the reason as soon as he got in the car. "Coach Holmgren and I went out for a beer today," his mother said, breaking into a smug smile that made Knute wonder if, instead of talking ice hockey, they'd declared true love.

"You did?" he asked.

She nodded. "He called me."

"You know you're both married?" Knute asked.

Mrs. Pescadoor braked hard. Turned and stared at her son. "Knute! What a thing to say to your mother!"

Knute shrugged and said he was sorry.

"*If you want to know*," she said, "he called me because you missed practice."

"I should have kept my mouth shut," Knute mumbled.

"What'd you say? I couldn't hear you."

He raised his voice. "I said I should have kept my mouth shut."

Mrs. Pescadoor began driving again. "You know what else Coach Holmgren said after we got together?"

Knute shook his head.

"After the second loss, Thursday evening, he went back and studied all my charts from the previous years and compared my figures with the statistics he's been keeping this year."

"Un-hunh."

"You wanna know what he found out?"

Knute nodded, not at all interested.

"Every player that's been with the team the last three years is doing at least 80 percent as well this year as his average. Except for you."

Knute's face wrinkled up and he looked at his mother sideways. "What are you talking about, Mom?" he asked sharply. When he'd called her he'd expected her to start crying or yelling, instead she had been very sweet. Then she'd started boasting about having had a beer with Mr. Holmgren. Who, theretofore, his mother had always criticized or made fun of. And then the two of them had decided it was all because of him that the team had lost the last two games?

"Here, listen," she said. "You take Doug. This is his sixth year with the team. You take his average the previous five seasons—how many goals he would normally have after six games. That number is fourteen. This year he only has twelve. So he's down a little, but he's still doing a little better than 80 percent of his average.

"But now you look at your statistics. You've been with White's a little over four years, and your average after six games for those first four years is four goals. But this year you don't have any. Which, you can see, is significantly less than 80 percent."

Knute was starting to get very angry. "It's also four goals," he said sharply. "And if I could have only scored those four goals in the last two games, we would have won one and tied the other. It's all my fault—that's what you're trying to tell me, right? Thanks a lot, Mom. Thanks a fucking lot. This is just what I wanted to hear tonight. How I am the reason White's is no longer unbeatable."

"Knute, Knute," his mother tried to say soothingly. "You don't understand. Coach Holmgren and I aren't trying to say at all that it's your fault. No. In fact Bob has decided it was *his* fault. He shouldn't have been playing kids on lines together based on how they did at the tryout; he should have been figuring out the *combinations* of players that were going to work the best. He wants you to play with Doug again. That's what he said."

She reached and patted his thigh. "Oh, Knute, I feel like I've told this to you the wrong way. I never meant for you to take it as criticism. I thought you'd think it was *good* news. That's what Bob thought too. The main thing is that we are going to get you and Doug together again. Isn't that great!"

Knute shook his head, slowly. Not so much disagreeing as confused. "Explain the 'we,'" he said.

She slapped the horn with the side of her fist. "I'm assistant coach again! Can you believe it? He wants me back on the bench during games, and he wants me to keep the statistics again. He says there's no way to figure out what the best combinations are unless we're constantly monitoring ourselves."

"I guess not," Knute said. So he was going to be back playing with Doug. It did seem that would be a kick, but . . . Basically, what he wanted to do was spend as much time as possible with Karen.

That Monday just before lunch, when he opened his locker he found a note from Karen saying she hoped he would come out to her house again the next Saturday. Only this time she wanted to listen to *him* play. Or they could play together.

He played in the game that Tuesday afternoon and went to

the Thursday afternoon practice. And on Saturday he again got up early, left his mother a note and rode out to Karen's house. He was there before eight, but not before his mother had called and told Karen's mother that she was coming out to get him. It was fine for him to play music with Karen, but not when he was supposed to be at hockey practice.

"Knute, this has got to stop and it's going to stop," were her first words after he got in the car. "Bob and I are working very hard to try and get White's back on the winning track. But we are only the coaches. We can't go out there on the ice and shoot the puck for you. And there's no way you're going to be any good in the games if you don't come to the practices. Now Bob and I have—"

"Can it, Mom," Knute said.

Mrs. Pescadoor applied the brakes again. "Knute Pescadoor! The way you talk to your mother these days!"

Knute crossed his arms on his chest. "Mom," he said. "I'm gonna give you a choice."

"What are you talking about?" she said, grimacing.

"Here's the choice. Either I'm going to play hockey only when *I* want to, or I'm not going to play at all."

His mother shook her head slowly. Knute had turned it into a test of strength. She stared at the steering wheel. He didn't really care about hockey, or Karen, so much as he needed to prove he was fifteen years old, his mother had no more power over him. "Goddamn it," she hissed. "I went through this when Nick Jr. was fifteen, I went through this when Anne was fifteen. I just don't have the strength to go through it a third time."

She turned, stared at Knute and spoke as calmly as she

229

could. "I don't want to have to fight you about this, Knute," she said. "Next year if you want to give up ice-skating forever, you have my permission. You have my blessing. But, at the beginning of this season, in signing up to play for White's you made a commitment to the team. And I think I speak for both Bob and myself when I say we hope you will find a way to keep that commitment."

Knute shrugged, said nothing.

"You think we're only interested in winning, don't you?" his mother asked.

"Oh no," Knute said and laughed.

His mother growled between clenched teeth, drove on.

Just before lunch on Monday Karen was waiting at his locker, and they sat together in a back corner of the cafeteria. He told her he was "fucking sick" of White's.

She touched his hand, looked into his eyes and said, "I know."

"So why can't I just fucking quit! My mother says I made a commitment—when? To who? To some fucking coach who can't even ice-skate?"

"Maybe you should just go to Mr. Holmgren and tell him you don't want to play anymore," Karen suggested.

In the locker room before the Tuesday afternoon game, Knute did just that. The coach had him sit down on the bench next to him, and he put his arm around him. "I know it's been a hard year, Knute," he said, "and I consider myself somewhat to blame for that. I busted in here like I knew it all, like I was going to take a team with a perfect record and make it even more perfect. I pushed your mother aside. I separated you from your friend. All that was wrong, Knute."

Knute closed his eyes. What was wrong was that Karen was down in his friend's basement playing her viola with his band, and he was sitting in a locker room about to play ice hockey. "I just want to stop," he said.

Mr. Holmgren patted him on the back. "You know your mother and I have talked a lot about you and your role on this team."

Knute nodded. "We believe you're essential," he said. "We can't do it without you."

Knute decided [half-heartedly] that he would give "them" [Coach Holmgren and his mother] one more chance. He'd play as hard as he could that afternoon. See if he could score a goal, try to get to "80 percent of his average."

White's won by a large margin. In the locker room afterward the kids were all talking about how they'd skated around this or that kid on the other team; they made jokes about how bad that other team was; told one another they were "awesome," "too tough."

Mr. Holmgren invited his mother in, put his arm around her and made a little speech about how now, with her back on the bench, White's was never going to lose another game ever.

Knute slipped out the door and walked home by himself. He told himself he was glad the team was happy, Mr. Holmgren was happy, his mother was happy. It wasn't that he hadn't scored a goal; that he'd mishandled every pass Doug had made to him; that kids had kept skating around him, beating him to the loose pucks. It was all those things and mainly—*he just didn't want to play anymore*.

And he didn't see why he had to. And he decided he wasn't going to. Ever again.

*

The next Saturday Knute again skipped practice and rode out to Karen's. His mother called again to say she was coming to get him, but this time he rode away before she got there. He rode to his brother and sister-in-law's house and, while they sat in their living room with their son watching cartoons on television, Knute broke into the garage and took a bag of the largest fireworks he could find.

He rode back to his house, stowed the fireworks behind the garage and went inside. His mother was waiting for him with a hefty new bicycle lock, and she got his bike and locked it to one of the aluminum posts for the front porch awning, telling him that when he had proven that he was capable of living up to his commitments, he would have the use of his bike back.

Knute went down to the basement and started playing the organ. Karen had said she wanted them to figure out a way to play a certain song, and so he started picking out the simple melody on the organ, first humming along, then singing. The song was about love and faithfulness; with a succession of metaphors a woman told how devoted she was to her lover, even though he wasn't famous or muscle-bound. Singing the words, thinking of both Karen and of the female singer who had recorded the song, Knute's eyes began to water. His fingers struck harder against the keyboard, he sang louder and louder. The guy wasn't famous or muscle-bound but he and his lover were happy. That was all that mattered.

A few hours later his mother called from the top of the stairs asking Knute if he would come up and help her, she had a lot of groceries. As they were opening the wayback of the station wagon, she apologized for having had to lock his bike up. She said she knew he must be very upset with her. Maybe it was her and Coach Holmgren's fault. She wanted them to still be friends. "And, to get our new friendship started on the right track! Da-da!" She overturned one of the bags on the counter, revealing two T-bone steaks. "Two serious T-bones, wouldn't you say? Set up the grill on the back patio. Bake up some potatoes. Sour cream next to. Whadda you say? Sounds pretty good, eh?"

Knute nodded. She was just lucky it was only her car he was going to get. He laughed to himself. It was probably impossible anyway. Mothers were probably like those starfish, or whatever they were, where you hack one arm off and another one grows back in its place.

Knute helped his mother prepare the dinner, did the dishes, played double solitaire and watched television with her. Around midnight when his mother went up to bed he went down to the basement, started playing the organ again, working with different arrangements of his and Karen's pop song.

Around one, his father came home and he invited Knute to come up and have a nightcap with him.

His father fixed himself a Scotch on the rocks, fixed Knute a root beer, and they went and sat at the dining room table.

"So, you really love playing that organ," Mr. Pescadoor said.

Knute shrugged. "I guess. I play it a lot."

"Your mother tells me you're in a band now?"

"Well, not really. I go over to a friend's house sometimes, and he's got an organ in his basement too, so we play there."

"I should get you one of those portable keyboards like jazz people are starting to use."

"That would be great!"

They sat quietly sipping their drinks, the dining room lights dimmed, the reflection of the flood lights gleaming on the frost-covered flagstones of the patio outside.

"Sure is good to get home every night," Mr. Pescadoor said.

"Yeah, it's nice and quiet?" Knute asked.

"Oh yeah. Some mornings I'll just be pulling out of the driveway, and this voice in the back of my head will say, 'Why, in God's name, are you doing this, Nicholas Pescadoor? You've already got too much money and property. Why do you want to drive an hour into the city every day and bust your ass to get dinner for strangers? Wander around from table to table asking kids you've never met before if it's their birthday. Asking their parents if they want another cocktail.'"

He laughed. "Just saying it out, I can hear how ridiculous it is."

Knute nodded. "So why don't you quit?"

His father laughed again. Sat back in his chair, crossed his legs. "Why don't I quit?" he said slowly. He jiggled the keys and change in his pants pocket. "You know what it is?" he asked.

Knute shook his head.

"It's too much fun. I have too goddamn much fun with my restaurants. What I've learned in all these years is that this is my idea of a good time. Making sure hundreds of people every night are fed promptly and courteously, and that I get twenty-five cents of every dollar they pay out—it's too ridiculous not to be fun."

Mr. Pescadoor stood up, took a last swig of his Scotch and set the glass down definitively on the table. Then, for a moment or two he looked at Knute, subconsciously wondering what kind of person his son was becoming, what kind of career might await him. "Boy I'm tired," he said, picked up the two glasses, took them into the pantry and loaded them into the dishwasher.

When he came back into the dining room he tapped Knute on the shoulder. "I hope you, Anne and Nick Jr. are as lucky as I have been," he said.

They went upstairs together, but unlike his father Knute did not get into bed. He sat by his door, keeping it open a crack, listening for his father to settle down. He waited another half-hour, then slipped out of his room and down the stairs.

First he got the key to the bike lock out of the kitchen drawer where his mother had put it. He unlocked his bike and rolled it a little ways down the street from the house. Then he went behind the garage and got the bag of firecrackers.

*

In his role as older brother educating his younger brother in the ways of the world, Nick Jr. had many times told Knute about a certain practical joke/act of vandalism that he had committed as a senior in high school. According to the story at least, in Nick Jr.'s senior year there had been a big football game between the local high school, which at that time was in first place in its league, and an inner-city team that was in first place in its league. The game was scheduled to be played in the Pescadoors' town, in the suburbs. And, Nick Jr. maintained, the night before the game he and some friends had driven into the city, and, by stringing together a lot of powerful firecrackers and slipping them into the gas lines, they had wiped out all the other school's buses. None of the other team's fans had been able to make it to the game; the players had had to come in carpools. And no one had ever found out who'd done it because they'd done such a professional job.

That night of his ninth-grade year Knute was hoping to eliminate his mother's station wagon and interrupt her life much as his brother had interfered with that opposing team; and, in later years, many times Knute pressed his brother to explain why, when their father went outside the next morning, the station wagon was in exactly the same condition it had been in the night before, except there was a string of undetonated fire-

236

works coming out of the gas tank and hanging down along the side.

"Moisture. It had to be moisture," his brother insisted. "At some point in the evening you must have set the bags in a puddle or something." He claimed that for years he had sold thousands of those particular fireworks, they were one of his most popular items—and no one besides Knute had ever claimed they didn't work. "The only thing I can see is that they got too wet and either your fuses didn't keep burning properly or your cylinders wouldn't detonate."

When Knute was in his twenties, he did some checking with his brother's friends, and he discovered that none of them could remember his brother ever blowing up any bus, inner-city or suburban. Nick Jr. had thrown a lot of eggs and water balloons, it appeared. At least once he had decorated the trees around the local high school with toilet paper. There was some story about how Knute's father had told Nick Jr. about a whorehouse in the inner city, and for weeks Nick Jr. and his friends had been planning to go there. But then they had ended up inviting their girlfriends to go with them, and as they were driving along the darker streets of the city someone . . . Some of Nick Jr.'s friends remembered that it was one of the girls, some remembered that it was one of the boys, who suggested they go to a hotel bar and listen to the piano player.

*

Late that night back when he was fifteen, Knute got a long piece of string, went out to his mother's car, pulled back the

237

little lid covering the gas cap and removed the cap. He dipped the string in the pipe until it seemed to be well soaked, then he sat on the back porch steps braiding the fireworks together with the string, just as his brother had explained it to him, at least half a dozen times.

As an adult he more than once reflected that it was only when he got completely wrapped up in his anger or frustration—violent desire—only then did he ever feel, in any real, animal way, alive. That night he carefully lowered his braid into the pipe along the back of his mother's car. He held the end out so he would have something to light.

He felt the cool dampness of the night air spreading through his lungs. He always liked the hum of the street lights late at night. He went back into the kitchen to get matches, came out, lit the string, ran for his bike and started pedaling as fast as he could for Karen's house.